SUSAN'S TRUTH

Six Sisters For Bear Creek Book 3

KATIE WYATT

ADA OAKLEY

RoyceCardiff

Copyright © 2021 by Katie Wyatt

Copyright © 2021 by Ada Oakley

All rights reserved.

No part of this book may be reproduced in any form or by any electronic or mechanical means, including information storage and retrieval systems, without written permission from the author, except for the use of brief quotations in a book review.

RoyceCardiff
Publishing House
WHOLESOME INSPIRATIONAL ROMANCE

Dear Reader,

It is our utmost pleasure and privilege to bring these wonderful stories to you. I am so very proud of our amazing team of writers and the delight they continually bring us all with their beautiful clean and wholesome tales of, faith, courage, and love.

What is a book's lone purpose if not to be read and enjoyed? Therefore, you, dear reader, are the key to fulfilling that purpose and unlocking the treasures that lie within the pages of this book.

NEWSLETTER SIGN UP GET FREE BOOKS!

http://katieWyattBooks.com/readersgroup

*THANK YOU FOR CHOOSING A
INSPIRATIONAL READS BY ROYCE CARDIFF
PUBLISHING HOUSE.*

Welcome and Enjoy!

CONTENTS

A PERSONAL WORD FROM KATIE	1
Chapter 1	3
Chapter 2	13
Chapter 3	23
Chapter 4	32
Chapter 5	40
Chapter 6	49
Chapter 7	59
Chapter 8	68
Chapter 9	77
Chapter 10	84
Chapter 11	94
Chapter 12	102
Chapter 13	110
Epilogue	128
ABOUT THE AUTHORS	136

A PERSONAL WORD FROM KATIE

I LOVE WRITING ABOUT THE OLD WEST AND THE trials, tribulations, and triumphs of the early pioneer women.

With strong fortitude and willpower, they took a big leap of faith believing in the promised land of the West. It was always not a bed of roses, however many found true love.

Most of the stories are based on some historical fact or personal conversations I've had with folks who knew something of that time. For example a relative of the Wyatt Earp's. I have spent much time out in the West camping hiking and carousing. I have spent countless hours gazing up at night thinking of how it must been back then.

Thank you for being a loyal reader.

Katie

✦

SIX SISTERS FOR BEAR CREEK

Book 1: Sadie's Adventure

Book 2: Emily's Dream Come True

Book 3: Susan's Truth

Book 4: Diane's Healing Heart

Book 5: Laura's New Family

Book 6: Helen's Hope

CHAPTER 1

January 1871

Susan Williams sighed and put her book down, open on her lap for what felt like the hundredth time this day alone. Her companion, although that was a strong word for the woman who held the ticket for the seat next to hers, was talking again.

"So...you're traveling out west to meet a man and marry him?" she asked.

Susan nodded. "Yes, Anna. As I have explained before, it is the way these things are done."

"But what if you don't like him?" Anna asked. She was at least a couple of years younger than Susan and still had the rounded features of those not yet chiseled by the world.

"Then I suppose I will have to make do or renege on our deal," Susan said. "But from his letters, Max Peterson is a lovely man. Two of my sisters are in Bear Creek already, and they have assured me he is a good sort with a steady job at the local bank. I don't imagine there will be any trouble."

"You have great faith," Anna said. "Did you pray hard for a husband? Although I suppose a beauty like you would never have to pray for that."

"You're too kind," Susan said. She was no beauty and knew it. She was shorter than her sisters, a little plump, and frankly, her long dark hair with golden-brown streaks that occurred naturally was her best feature. Her eyes were olive, and her face far rounder than that of any of her five sisters. No, she was no beauty, but she didn't put much stock in that sort of thing anyway. No woman died old and beautiful. The world took that away. It was far better to make her mind formidable. That was something she could treasure.

"I will never find a husband; my father said as much," Anna continued. She was wringing her handkerchief again, and Susan suspected there would be more tears. So far, her journey west had been punctuated by hours of consoling this poor soul.

Anna had confided that her father was sending her west to her aunt, who lived in Salem, Oregon, in the hopes she would be able to make her fit for marriage. What was wrong with the young lady, Susan couldn't tell. She was polite and pretty, if a little soggy, and seemed perfectly capable of holding an average conversation. She embroidered when not crying and confided she could play the piano with relative success. Since most men only wanted a pretty face that could sew and entertain, Susan was at a loss as to what the problem was.

"As I have said repeatedly," she said in a tone far snappier than she intended, "I can't see why you would have a problem getting a husband if that is what you want."

Anna looked around. The ladies' car was mostly empty. Their traveling companions were no doubt stretching their legs with a walk of the train or in the dining car, where coffee and sweet buns were served at all hours.

Finding the coast clear, Anna seemed to feel confident enough to confide in Susan.

"It's because of my medical condition," Anna said. "I have a nervous stomach. When I get worked up..." she leaned closer to Susan. "I get gassy. It's quite terrible. My father is convinced that I will never make a good match because I get too nervous when meeting someone, and then things go oh so wrong. He's hoping my aunt can find a cure or calm me down."

Susan could imagine how those meetings in the parlor went. She tried not to smile.

"Is Bear Creek far from Salem?" Anna asked.

"According to my sisters, it's about a half-day's ride," Susan said. "But Anna, dear, shouldn't you be getting all packed up? The next stop is Salem, and we should be just about there."

Anna nodded. "It's just you've been so kind. May we write to each other?"

Perhaps her letters would be less damp. "Certainly," Susan said. "I don't know what my address will be, but perhaps you could give me your aunt's?"

Anna smiled and, rummaging in her bag, found a little scrap of paper and jotted down the address. She thrust it at Susan, looking a good deal happier than she'd looked for a while. Susan took the paper and placed it in her book.

"There, Kierkegaard will keep it safe," she said.

"I know you told me who he is, but I've forgotten," Anna confided. She turned to her packing.

Susan sighed. "He was a philosopher and wrote about faith and Christianity and man's relationship to God. It's very interesting."

"It sounds complicated," Anna said.

"Oh, it's not that bad," Susan said. "I can lend you a book if you like, and you can see if you like it."

Anna smiled. "Thank you for the offer, but I'm far too woolly-headed for that. Father always said I was too silly for much."

"I think your father sold you short," Susan said. "My father encouraged me to learn. Always. Maybe, when you're settled in Salem, we can see about working out just how woolly-headed you actually are. You might be surprised."

"All right," Anna said, although she sounded doubtful.

The train pulled into the Salem station just as Anna packed the last of her things. She was weepy again as she said farewell to Susan.

"Don't forget to write," she said.

Susan nodded. "I will as soon as I arrive in Bear Creek and find out where I'll be living. Max had me send my letters to his bank, but I don't think I can take that liberty."

Anna smiled through her tears and hugged Susan to her. "You are wonderful. I'm so glad we met."

Susan smiled. "Me too." Anna reminded her of her sister Emily in a way, and she was always fond of Em. Perhaps another silly woman in her life might be a good thing.

With that, Anna left the train and disappeared among the crowd on the Salem platform.

All distraction gone, Susan picked up *Fear and Trembling* again and began to read. It was truly fascinating how Kierkegaard saw the world and humanity's relationship with God. Her own relationship with said deity was on the rocks. They'd had a falling out after God took her dear papa to heaven, and while Susan definitely believed in the Lord, she was, in a word, angry.

Even through her anger, she was still drawn to trying to understand that most compelling of questions: why? And so, she read the Bible and philosophy and anything else that might, in some way, give her an answer.

"Next stop, Bear Creek and Crystal Lake!" the conductor called as he walked the length of the train.

Susan sighed. Finally. The day was waning, and so her first view of her new home would be through the colors of sunset. Emily would find it romantic. Susan thought it was fitting. The end of something should be colored in oranges and reds and pinks. With the clouds streaking the sky and the ground still dotted with banks of unmelted snow, Oregon was quite pretty. So far.

The train pulled into the station. It seemed a sturdily built platform, open to the elements, with no roof. Good thing it wasn't raining. There was a crowd of people on the platform, no doubt waiting for their friends and family to disembark.

Susan wasted no time when the train stopped. She had her bags all ready and was one of the first to set foot on the platform. Of course, "where to now?" was a pressing question since she had no idea what Max Peterson looked like.

She scanned the crowd. There was a single man in a hat and large coat who might be Mr. Peterson. She watched him, but he waved to another man and they left together. Then she spotted a man who also might be Max. He was tall and had the collar of his coat up. She thought it was him until she saw the two little girls holding his hands. No, Max had no children.

Another man looked promising until a woman walked up to him and kissed him passionately in public, which Susan found highly inappropriate. And then there were no people left.

Mr. Peterson—calling him Max seemed a little forward—must have forgotten. No problem. She would make her own way. Susan picked up her suitcase and carpetbag and began to make her way to the stairs.

"Miss Susan Williams?"

She turned. "Yes?"

It was the man with the two little girls holding his hands.

"Max Peterson," he said with a little bow made awkward by the children.

Susan didn't know what to say.

"I'm sorry," he said. "Wasn't sure how to do this."

"Do what?" Susan asked, her chest constricting as though it were in a vise.

"Well, these are my twin daughters, Alyssa and Cassia," he said. He looked nervous and hopeful.

"No," Susan said, shaking her head. This couldn't be happening. "Max Peterson doesn't have children. He would have told me."

"I didn't think you'd come if I told you before you got here, but the girls are just darling," Max said.

"I see," Susan said. She nodded. Of course, this had been too good to be true. Children? Quite the oversight on his part.

"I am sorry," Mr. Peterson said. He looked sad.

It made Susan feel something so alien she didn't know what to do about it. She was confused. What was happening? She had so many questions.

"And their mother?" she asked.

"Left me, I told you in the letters," Mr. Peterson said.

Susan nodded. "Well, you know one untruth can often lead to more."

The children were eyeing her like foxes eyeing a rabbit for dinner.

There was only one logical recourse. "Take me to my sisters. Now!" she demanded.

"But Miss Williams..." he said, looking very upset.

"Please," she said.

Something seemed to melt in him, and he nodded.

Susan was finally able to draw breath.

CHAPTER 2

The ride out to the farm was a quiet one. Susan was in no mood to talk, and after a few failed attempts at conversation, Mr. Peterson stopped trying to engage her. Instead, he and his children spoke, although what the twins were saying was beyond Susan. She could hardly understand a word. Their pronunciation was awful.

With the sun kissing the horizon, they finally reached the farm and rode up the long drive. At the top of it was a large farmhouse with whitewashed walls and a slate roof. Across from the house were a barn and a paddock with several wooly sheep.

"Well, here you are," Mr. Peterson said glumly. "Would you like me to wait for you?"

"Good heavens, no!" Susan said, frowning. "Whatever

for?"

"I thought you were popping in to see your sisters," Mr. Peterson said.

Susan sighed. She should explain herself. "Mr. Peterson..."

"Call me Max, please," he said.

"No. Not yet. I don't know who you are. Leaving out that you have two daughters was a rather large omission, and frankly, I'm nervous about what else you decided I didn't need to know," Susan said harshly.

He moved back as though she'd hit him.

"I'm sorry," Susan said, softening at the look of hurt on his face. "I just need a little time and space to think this through. I assume you want me to look after the children and that's the real reason you were looking for a wife?"

Reluctantly, Mr. Peterson nodded. "They need a mother. But I am also looking for companionship... not necessarily romance. Just someone to talk to..."

Susan bit her lip and nodded. "All of this would have been nice to know beforehand. I'm sure you can understand my reticence at becoming an instant mother. It is a massive responsibility, and you haven't given me time to decide if it's what I want." She swallowed. "I will spend the night at my sisters', and then we can talk in the morning. Is that fair?"

He nodded. "All right. I can see this was more of a shock than I expected it to be. Take your time, Miss Williams."

She climbed down from the cart. One of the little girls, who were almost completely identical with dark hair and their father's blue eyes, said something that Susan didn't catch.

"Alyssa says she hopes you change your mind," Mr. Peterson translated for her.

Susan smiled at the little girl. "I will certainly keep that in mind. Well, you'd better be off. I assume you have some way to go to get them home?"

Mr. Peterson nodded. He climbed down and helped her with her bags, which he placed on the ground.

"I can carry them in for you," he offered.

The open willingness to please her made her smile. Susan took her bags in hand. "No need. I can manage. Will you be at the bank tomorrow? I imagine I should wait until evening to come and see you so that we can talk?"

Mr. Peterson nodded. "Evening would be best. However, I will come here."

With that settled, Susan walked to the back door. There were several pairs of muddy boots she had to step around to mount the steps. She raised her hand and knocked.

The door opened instantly to reveal Sadie and Emily standing in the doorway. They opened their arms with screeches of joy.

"You're here!" Emily cried, wrapping her arms around Susan and almost smothering her.

Sadie hugged them both, turning it into a group hug, and then stopped. "Hold on. Where is Mr. Peterson going?"

"I'm staying here tonight," Susan said. "If you'll have me."

"What happened?" Sadie asked, her hands instantly going to her hips. *Just like Mother*, Susan thought.

"Can I at least come in before spilling the beans?" Susan asked.

"Of course," Emily said. She took the carpetbag. "Come on, Sadie. Help Susan in."

Reluctantly watching the Petersons disappear down the drive, Sadie picked up Susan's suitcase and followed them inside, closing the door behind her.

They sat Susan at the long wooden table in the kitchen, which smelled of Sadie's famous beef stew, and Emily sat with her. Sadie began to add to the pots boiling on the range.

"We'll have to make more dinner," she said. "Between your appetite and Tony's, there won't be enough for the rest of us."

Susan sighed. "I don't eat that much anymore."

"Oh, give her a break, Sadie," Emily said. "She's having a trying day. Can't you see that?" She turned back to Susan. "Come on, dear one, tell me what happened."

With no embellishment at all, Susan told her sisters what had happened to make her react like she had. Mr. Peterson had lied. Well, not lied as such; he'd never said he didn't have children, but he also failed to mention them.

"And you both didn't mention them either," she said, frowning. "Surely they didn't spontaneously pop into existence yesterday."

"No," Sadie said. "They're about three or four years old."

Susan glared at her sister and made a "well, there you go" gesture.

"I'm sorry," Emily said, taking Susan's hands in hers. "I thought Max had told you in the letters that he had Alyssa and Cassia. It didn't cross my mind to mention them in my letters home because...well... there's so much else going on here. I mean, we've had sick sheep, and it's almost lambing time, and..." she sighed. "I don't think it's a good excuse, but we assumed you knew."

Susan sighed and squeezed her sister's hand. "I thought it would be something like that. Don't worry. I'm not upset with you. I just needed some time to think."

"So, you'll be heading to Max's house tomorrow then?" Sadie asked, stirring a pot that bubbled, emitting a delicious smell.

"I don't know," Susan confided.

Sadie turned, ladle in hand. She shook it at Susan. "It's the kids, isn't it? You have never liked children. Ever since Laura and Helen were born, you have hated little children. Haven't you?"

Susan was taken aback. It sounded like she was some child-loathing monster to hear Sadie talk like that. She'd never taken herself to be anything of the sort. She was a scholar and therefore had no time for children other than as students.

"Oh, she doesn't hate them," Emily said, frowning angrily at Sadie. "She's just strict. Right, Sue? I mean, you've worked with children as a governess, haven't you?"

Susan nodded.

"And how well did that end?" Sadie asked, eyeing her sister.

"Oh, they were unreasonable," Emily said. "Firing you because you thought their daughter should know arithmetic." She clicked her tongue in disapproval.

"Em, please!" Sadie said. "They fired her because she was too strict on the children. Poor little things were in tears all the time. Their mother couldn't console them when she was done with them."

"They shouldn't have glued my book shut!" Susan protested.

"It was just a book," Sadie said, turning back to the stew.

"It was by one of the world's greatest minds! Pages with Frederick Nietzsche's words on them should not be drawn on and painted over and then glued shut!" Susan yelled.

"Well, now, I thought I heard a new female voice yelling in my kitchen."

A man stepped into the room through the back door. He was tall with dark blond hair and a stubbly beard. He smiled and held out a hand to Susan.

"Hi, I'm Tony, Emily's husband, and you have to be Susan," he said, shaking her hand.

Susan nodded. "Why do I have to be?"

"Because you look like them," he said, indicating her sisters. "Welcome to Bear Creek. I trust your journey was pleasant."

"It was, thank you," Susan said.

The door opened again, and another man entered. He was shorter than Tony but unmistakably his brother.

"And you must be Kyle," Susan said, offering her hand as he approached.

"Susan, I'm guessing?" he asked. "Well, this is a full house. I thought you were staying at Max's place, or did I get that wrong?"

"No, Susan changed her mind," Sadie said before launching into her version of events as she dished up dinner for them all.

As they all ate the delicious rice and stew Sadie had made, they discussed Susan's predicament. Tony and Emily were on her side; however, Sadie and Kyle seemed to think she was overreacting.

"Max has had it hard," Kyle said around some stew. "His first wife, Holly, had the twins and then ran off about a month later. He's been raising them on his own."

"On his own?" Emily asked. "You mean with a string of nannies."

Kyle shrugged. "Same thing."

"Why a string of them?" Susan asked.

"Well, between us and the bright blue sky," Sadie said, "although perfect angels when their father is around... apparently the girls turn into little monsters with the hired help."

Susan shuddered. "I don't think I'm the right person."

"Well, you'll have to be," Sadie said, blowing on her spoonful of stew. "Not a great many options for husbandless women out this way."

"And he's a real good man," Tony said. "Give him a chance."

When dinner was over, Susan helped wash up and then followed Emily upstairs to the guest bedroom. It was bright, warm, and comfortable, with a cheerful fire in the grate.

"There, I hope you'll sleep well," Emily said. She hugged Susan. "It's good to have you here."

"Thanks," Susan said. "For everything."

Emily nodded. "I find praying on a problem helps me no end. I know you are angry with God, but give it a try. It might work."

Susan thanked her again, and when Emily left the room, she sagged onto the bed. What would Kierkegaard do in this situation? She doubted he'd ever been in anything like it. Well, she'd sleep on it and see how she felt in the morning. The one thing she *wouldn't* do was pray.

CHAPTER 3

The next day dawned gray and overcast. It was surprisingly cold. Susan dressed in a gray woolen dress with her dark green velvet jacket.

Things on the farm happened early, and by the time she went down to the kitchen, Emily and Sadie were already eating bowls of porridge.

"Did you sleep well?" Emily asked as she entered.

Susan nodded. "I did."

"Have you decided what you're doing?" Sadie asked.

Susan nodded again as she spooned porridge into a bowl. "I have."

"And?" Sadie asked.

Not liking her sister's tone one bit, Susan smiled and spooned sugar into her bowl. She followed it with cream and ate in silence.

Emily watched them both like a nervous rabbit watching two cats to see who would attack first. But neither did.

Susan helped with the dishes and then spent the day around the farm with her sisters while Tony and Kyle tended the sheep. Washing clothes, hanging them before the fire in the kitchen to dry, and mending and sewing took her back to their apartment in Boston. Those had been hard but enjoyable times when all the sisters had lived together.

In some way, Susan wished it could be like that again, with everyone knowing their place in the world. Even she had a place. Tutoring the neighborhood children in arithmetic, grammar, and reading had been her only way to bring in money. At first, many had thought her presumptuous, wanting to help boys with their studies too. However, when she proved herself perfectly knowledgeable, their mothers had been happy to hand over the pittance she asked. Many a boy had done well enough to ensure higher education at any institution of his choice.

Out here in the middle of nowhere, Susan wasn't sure where she fit in. She knew she wasn't traditional wife material. She'd never gravitated to their mother like the others had. Father had been her rock and her comforter. She'd loved his active mind and his ability to make even the most complex ideas relatable for her.

Oh, how she missed their evenings in front of the parlor fire, reading and discussing the day. She'd learned so much. She wished he were here so she could speak to him.

All too soon it was late afternoon and then evening, and before Susan was entirely ready, she could hear the clip-clop of hooves on the drive.

Max Peterson soon sat across from Susan at the kitchen table, looking drawn and tired. His dark hair was ruffled as though he'd run agitated fingers through it, and his blue eyes looked dark and apprehensive. Had she done that to him? Caused that much distress?

"You look more settled," Max said.

"Yes, I feel better," Susan said. "How are you?"

"Well..." he said, clasping his hands together where they lay on the table. "It's hard to say. I suppose I am desperately curious as to your decision. If it helps, the girls said they liked you."

"How could they possibly know after such a short time?" Susan asked.

"They're three," he said as though that explained everything.

Perhaps she should make it clearer that her experience with little children was limited. Although now didn't seem to be the time.

"Be that as it may," she said, "I have a proposition for you."

He sat up straighter. "All right. What do you propose?"

"We are strangers," she said flatly. "I think it's obvious that letters exchanged for a few months didn't tell us much about each other. However, I am willing to marry you."

He looked relieved.

"It will obviously be a business relationship for the foreseeable future. I will care for the girls, and I would like to be their educator. I'm sure you agree that the bond between parent and child can't be forced, and since we're strangers, this will take time.

Please don't force it. I would appreciate the room to navigate the relationship on my own with them."

He frowned for a moment and then nodded. "All right. So, you will take care of my girls and treat them with kindness?"

She nodded. "Of course. I'm strict but never cruel."

"That is so true!" Emily poked her head into the kitchen, and they both turned to look at her. "It's true. Susan is a lovely person under all that starch!" Her piece said, Emily turned scarlet and made a hasty retreat.

Susan felt awkward at her sister's words, and she was horrified to find that her cheeks were heating up. Why couldn't Emily ever keep her nose out of people's affairs?

"All right. And what would you like in return?" Max asked. "After all, I'm getting a version of what I wanted from this relationship. What is it you want?"

This was it. The moment where Susan would see what Mr. Max Peterson was truly made of. With her heart thumping in her chest, she looked him right in his blue eyes and said, "I want to be able to continue with my studies. Philosophy is fascinating, and I don't think I can live without my books and the time to explore them."

For a moment she thought she'd gone too far. Max's face seemed to crack as he regarded her. His lips, not too full but not thin either, began to pull in a straight line.

Oh dear, she thought. *I've pushed him too far.*

And then the corners of his mouth began to tilt upwards, and she realized he was smiling.

"Is that all you want?" he asked. "Time to read?"

Susan nodded. "Yes. Well, room and board as well, and the means to support myself."

Max dropped his gaze to the tabletop. "Kyle warned me that the Williams women were formidable, but I had no idea what he meant until now. You have yourself a deal." He looked her in the eye and held out his hand.

Susan was glad to see the levelheaded part of him that she had seen in the letters wasn't a lie. She accepted his hand and gave it a hearty shake. "We are in agreement."

"Yes, we are," he said. "Will you be coming home with me?"

She nodded. "Yes, I believe my sisters would love me to leave. I think my surprise visit has not endeared me to them. You do have a guest room, right?"

Max nodded. "Certainly, and we can get married tomorrow. The local preacher is always on hand to perform ceremonies."

Susan nodded.

With that settled, she went upstairs to fetch her bags. When she came back down, she found her sisters speaking to Max. They were both smiling.

"If you have any trouble with Susan," Sadie said, eyeing her. "Feel free to send her back to Boston, care of our sister Diane."

"Oh, you wouldn't!" Susan snapped. "Care of Diane?" She was outraged until Sadie burst into laughter, and Susan realized it was a joke.

"Oh, very funny, Sadie," Susan grumbled. "Come on, Max, let's go." She walked to the back door, where she hugged Emily. "Good luck living with her on your doorstep forever."

"It's a penance, but I can bear it," Emily said with a chuckle. "You take care, and if you need anything, you know where we are."

Susan thanked them, Sadie included, and left with Max.

The ride into town was not long, probably about half an hour, and the scenery, although seen in the dying light of the sun, was lovely, green, and lush. Susan had always loved the outdoors, so long as she could experience them through the window. There was a lot of outdoors here. One more thing to get used to.

Max Peterson's house was in town. It was around the corner from the bank and down a street lined with large houses. They all had front yards and white picket fences. The warm glow of candles in windows spilled out into the darkening evening and reminded Susan of the neighborhood her family had lived in before the tragedy.

It had been similar to this. A town house in a good neighborhood. She didn't remember too much about it, only being ten or eleven when everything had changed. But she remembered the yards and the windows.

They pulled up to a house, and Max jumped down off the cart and opened the gate. He drove the cart around to the back of the house, where there was a small stable for the horse. He helped Susan down and then handed the horse to a young boy.

"This is Roger," Max said. "He helps me with Rainbow."

"Rainbow?" she asked.

"The girls named the horse," he said.

Roger was a small creature in a brown coat and boots who nodded to her before disappearing with the horse.

With her bags in his hands, Max led her to the back door and opened it. "Welcome home," he said.

Susan took a deep breath, and with her resolve set, she stepped through the doorway.

CHAPTER 4

Meeting the family officially that night was nerve-wracking for Susan. The girls, Alyssa and Cassia, were well ensconced with the housekeeper, Mrs. Jemima Potts, who was an older lady with grown children of her own. She cleaned and cooked for the family, which Susan was thrilled about, not being much of a cook and even less of a housekeeper.

Mrs. Potts greeted Susan warmly and, gathering up her coat from the hook by the kitchen door, gave the little girls at the kitchen table quite a stern look. "Now you be good," she said.

The girls smiled around their spoonfuls of stew and nodded, and Mrs. Potts disappeared through the back door and out into the night.

It turned out that Max had a lovely beagle cross

terrier called Bunny who simply adored Susan from the moment she set foot in the house. The dog followed her around like she was a treat on legs.

All that remained was the children. Both girls smiled, but Susan knew enough about children to know that didn't mean a thing. They could smile now and scream the next second. Children were mercurial.

That night she and Max ate the delicious stew that Mrs. Potts had left for them at the kitchen table, and as the dinner conversation progressed, Susan's ear became more attuned to the children. Little children, still learning to speak properly, were often hard to understand, and the fact that Cassia sucked her left thumb incessantly made her words almost impossible to make out. However, with some careful listening, Susan began to hear the words. They would need elocution lessons for certain. Luckily, she was an experienced teacher and would have them speaking properly in no time.

When dinner was finished, Max helped Susan get the girls in bed. They shared a room at the end of the upstairs hall. It was decorated in powder blues and delicate pinks, which Susan thought suitable. The girls had twin beds set against the near wall so that both girls could see out of the room's one window, which lay opposite.

All neatly washed and dressed by Mrs. Potts, they climbed in bed, insisted their daddy read to them, and then went to sleep with no fuss at all, Cassia still sucking that thumb. Her teeth had clearly been pushed quite far forward, and the thumb showed signs of having been sucked for years. Susan would have to work hard to get her to stop.

When the children were asleep, Max showed her to her room, which was right next door. It was a bright room decorated in pale yellow and green. It, too, had a window that looked out over the backyard.

"I hope you'll be comfortable," he said.

"It's wonderful," Susan said, and it was. There was little furniture—only a closet, bed, washbasin, and a desk, but she needed nothing else. If she stayed in the room long, she might get herself a set of shelves for her books, but other than that, it was perfect. And it was hers. She didn't have to share with Laura, who snored all night long. That was a blessing.

She slept surprisingly well that night and woke fresh. Mrs. Potts was in already and making porridge for breakfast when Susan went downstairs. Max was sipping coffee at the kitchen table.

"Did you sleep well?" he asked, folding the paper he'd been reading and putting it down.

Susan nodded. "I did. Thank you. And you?"

"Yes," he said. "Have a seat and some coffee if you like."

Susan helped herself to a mug and took a seat opposite him at the table.

"I was thinking we should go to the church first this morning and get the wedding out of the way. Then I will head on to work. Mr. Morgan, my manager, is aware of the situation," Max said. "So, I can be a little late. Does that sound right to you? It will give you the rest of the day."

"Sounds perfect," Susan said, thankful she wasn't like her sisters and had never spent any time dreaming about her wedding. A quick wedding and then on with things seemed the most efficient way to do this.

They ate their breakfast and left the children in Mrs. Potts' care.

The church was not far from the house, and they could walk there in the crisp morning air. A frost had formed during the night, and although the sky was clear except for a few tattered white clouds, it was still bracingly cold.

The minister was an old man with gray hair and spectacles. He peered at them through the glasses and nodded his understanding. "Yes, yes," he said. "I take it you don't want the long version, just the vows?"

Max looked at Susan, who nodded. "If possible," he said. "Although I think a prayer to bless the marriage might be welcome." He glanced her way again, but Susan made no gestures. She wasn't sure how Max's relationship with God was. They hadn't gotten to that yet.

"All right," the minister said.

And in the blink of an eye, it was all over, and Susan Williams became Susan Peterson. Max kissed her cheek. The touch of his lips on her skin had an odd effect on her. She felt her pulse race, and gooseflesh erupt on her arms and legs as though she'd been exposed to a sudden draft.

She smiled at him, and he returned the smile, his dark blue eyes shining. Wearing their new wedding bands, which Max had supplied, they stepped out into the day.

Bear Creek was a busy place, with people going about their business. It was mostly people heading to the trader, the apothecary, the bathhouse, or the bank, it seemed to Susan. A fair few seemed to be wandering about aimlessly. Susan noted several children out playing a game in an open patch of ground.

"Shouldn't they be at school?" she asked.

Max nodded as they walked across the street, heading to the bank. "Yes, they should. However, some parents don't want their children walking halfway to Crystal Lake in this weather. Some of the roads and bridges are dangerous if there's ice."

"Oh," she said. "Is that the only school?"

He nodded. "Well, I must get to work. We can talk this evening?"

She nodded, half expecting another kiss on the cheek. They were married, after all; however, Max held out his hand to her. After a moment's hesitation, she took it, and they shook. He seemed to want to say something else but stopped himself, smiled, and removing his hat from his head, went into the bank.

Watching him go inside, Susan breathed in the icy air and turned up the collar of her coat. It was time to head back to the house and see what she could achieve with Alyssa and Cassia.

It felt good to officially be a wife. Although it was a stupid mental construct, it was true; an unmarried woman had endless trouble. At least now, so long as Max lived up to his end of their agreement, Susan had a certain amount of freedom. She could study and teach, and things would be fine.

When she reached the house, she noted that Bunny was in the front yard and seemed agitated.

"What is it, girl?" she asked, reaching over the low fence and patting the little dog's head lovingly. They'd snuggled the previous night, and Susan felt she and Bunny were good friends.

As she went in through the gate, Bunny hopped and jumped to the door, whining. Picking up her skirts, Susan jogged to the house, nearly tripping over the excited dog. She wrenched the front door open and went in.

That's when she heard muffled screaming. After a short search, she noticed it was coming from the hall. Another search and she found a door under the stairs. A large brass key stood in the lock. Susan turned it, and Mrs. Potts and a broom and some pails burst out, making Susan take several steps backward.

"Where are they?" she roared. "Those little devils! They've gone too far this time! I'll tan their hides, mark my words!"

Susan stared, open-mouthed. The housekeeper's face was a horrible brick red, and she was breathing like a wounded ox. But how had she ended up locked in what was clearly a broom closet? What had happened since Susan and Max left the house?

Pushing past the still-bewildered Susan, the housekeeper charged into the kitchen.

Concerned, Susan followed her. "Mrs. Potts? What is going on?"

But the housekeeper said nothing. She seemed transfixed to the spot. If Susan was given to flights of wild imagination, she might have thought a gorgon hid in the kitchen and had turned Mrs. Potts to stone, because the woman was motionless.

Following the housekeeper's gaze, Susan felt her mouth slide open as her heart stopped. The sight in the kitchen was beyond anything she could have expected.

CHAPTER 5

"Apricot jam," Susan said, sucking her finger, which she'd used to pick up some of the stuff coating the kitchen.

The twins giggled. They were covered in it. So were the ceiling, the floor, the kitchen table, and several kitchen cupboards.

Susan had sent Mrs. Potts into the parlor. At the sight of her lovely kitchen dripping sugary treats, the housekeeper had lost her mind. It was far safer if she had a lie-down. Susan could handle this. She was quite certain.

"Yummy," Alyssa said. She was about an inch taller than Cassia, and her eyes were a darker blue.

"Is that why you locked Mrs. Potts in the closet under the stairs?" Susan asked. She had them standing in the scullery. Two jam-covered horrors with bright smiles, as though they had done nothing wrong.

"Was locking her in an accident?" Susan asked. "Did you know what would happen if you turned the key?"

Two heads shook. "Wanted jam," Cassia said, her thumb not in her mouth for once but rather running down a strand of jam-covered hair. "Yummy."

"Meanie said no," Alyssa added.

"Meanie! Meanie!" they chanted.

"All right! That's more than enough," Susan said, using her stern-yet-still-friendly voice. Her temper threatened to flare up, but she would get nothing from them if she allowed that to happen.

"Girls, I understand that you wanted jam, but if Mrs. Potts says no, then it's no. Do you understand?" she asked, regarding them sternly.

The girls frowned and stuck out their tongues. They blew raspberries at her.

"That's enough!" she said. "Do you think your father would be pleased?"

At the mention of Max, both girls looked firmly at the floor, their little hands finding each other's and gripping tightly.

Susan's anger waned and she softened. These children had been through a rough time. Having their mother leave when they were very small, and then a parade of different nannies and other minders...it couldn't have been easy. She would have to be a steadfast, stable influence in their lives. Someone they could trust, who they knew cared for them. To be that, she would have to keep her temper.

"Come on, let's clean up the mess," Susan said gently.

"Don't want to," Alyssa said, raising a small, defiant chin.

"Well, you have to," Susan said firmly. "I don't know where the cleaning things are or where anything goes. You'll have to help me. And we can't leave the kitchen looking like this. Your father will be very upset if we do."

"Don't want to," Alyssa repeated. Cassia stayed silent.

"Did you know that you're both named after flowers?" Susan asked, taking them by the hand and leading them to the sink, where she began to fill it with water from the pump. "Alyssa, your name comes from the sweet asylum flower, and Cassia, yours is from the cassia plant, which smells like cinnamon."

The girls stared at her.

"We're flowers?" Alyssa asked.

Susan nodded, wetting a cloth and starting to wipe their faces and hands, getting the sticky jam off. "Yes, you both are. And you know that flowers are wonderful, friendly things, right?"

"Flowers got fairies," Cassia offered, and her thumb rose to her mouth.

Susan was tempted to stop her, but she felt that now wasn't the time. She needed to win them over first. "That's right," she said. "Now tell me. In the stories your daddy reads to you at night, are the fairies friendly?"

They nodded.

"Do you think the fairies would like flowers which were unkind or naughty?"

Two heads shook "no."

"Well, then, I think we need to work hard to clean up so the fairies don't think you're mean flowers and refuse to come and play with you," Susan said.

The twins exchanged worried looks and nodded. "'kay," Alyssa said.

It took a half hour to clean everything up, and when they were done, the girls went into the parlor and apologized to Mrs. Potts. The housekeeper, looking more like her usual self, spread her arms and enveloped them both in a hug.

"Right, now I'll make you jam sandwiches for lunch," she said.

The twins shook their heads. "Yuck! No more jam!" they yelled.

Susan laughed and shooed them upstairs to change their sticky clothes and wash the rest of the jam off. Once they were neat, tidy, and dressed properly, she took them out into the yard to play. Bunny was thrilled they were outside, and she gave up sniffing the grass to run and play fetch with a stick the girls took turns throwing for her.

Watching them from the porch, Susan noted that when alone, the girls were quite calm and pleasant.

Bored with playing fetch, the girls eventually came running over and asked Susan to play tag. She agreed, and for a while they ran around, trying to catch her.

The game broke the ice between them, and soon they were laughing and cheering.

Mrs. Potts appeared on the porch, wiping her hands on her apron. "All right, you lot!" she called. "Lunch!"

Susan ushered the children inside, where they found boiled eggs and toast, cheese slices, and an apple each for lunch. They ate, talking happily, and then Susan took the girls upstairs for a nap. They were tired and fell asleep with little trouble.

Thinking she would pass the time reading, Susan went to her room, lay down on the bed with *Fear and Trembling,* and began to read.

She woke with Alyssa and Cassia standing over her.

"Oh my goodness!" she cried, sitting up. Her book tumbled from her chest and landed on the floor with a thump. The light had changed. It had turned dull, and the sky outside was slate gray with clouds. "How long was I asleep?"

The twins shrugged.

She blinked. "Right, we should go and do something."

They smiled, and Cassia handed Susan her book. "What you wanna do?"

"Well, I thought we could try some drawing. Do you have slates and colored chalks?" she asked.

The girls shook their heads.

"No matter, let's go outside and draw in the sand in the yard," she said. She would have to get them slates. Perhaps the trader had some. It might be a fun outing to take the girls on.

Drawing in the dirt sounded entertaining to the girls, so they went down to the yard, and after finding suitable bits of stick, Susan had them drawing. At first, she let them doodle, drawing whatever they liked. This turned out to mostly be scribbles and flowers and some oddly shaped things Cassia insisted were bugs. Susan tried to copy their drawings with some success, and then after a while, she had them copy hers. From her days as a governess, she'd discovered that the best way to keep children interested in their lessons was to make them think they were playing. She turned it into a game, and they got points for copying her drawings, which were shapes, circles, squares, triangles, and the like. The girls chattered and laughed as they tried to copy them.

This worked well for a while, until things dissolved into chaos as would always happen with small children. Cassia laughed, drawing mustaches on everything, and Alyssa spent her time trying to balance her stick between her puckered lips and her nose.

Susan laughed with them until they became restless and she needed to find something else to keep them occupied.

"Why don't you show me around the backyard?" Susan asked in a moment of inspiration.

The girls nodded eagerly and took her by the hand, dragging her around the side of the house. The backyard was rather overgrown. Apart from the outhouse, the stable, and the washhouse where the family's large tin bath was kept, the rest of the garden was forest.

Susan was a little apprehensive of going into the forest, but the girls showed no fear, and Bunny was bounding around, looking excited to have them all outside. At this point the forest was thin, the pine trees spread apart, and other plants had filled in.

There was a path through the trees that led about ten yards up to what looked like a log cabin.

"What's that?" Susan asked.

"A little house," Alyssa said.

"Does anyone live there?" Susan asked.

The girls shook their heads and took her right up to it. It was covered in cobwebs and dirt, but the door opened when they turned the handle, and they stepped inside with no fear. Soon she could see why. The sparse furniture was covered in dust sheets, but the girls had made themselves a little house in the middle of the room, and their dolls and toys were all over the place. Clearly, they liked to play here. This gave Susan an idea.

CHAPTER 6

That evening at dinner, Susan raised the subject of the cabin out back in the garden.

"Is it being used for anything?" she asked.

Max frowned and cut his chicken breast into smaller pieces. "Not that I know of," he said. "It was our first house, while this one was being built. Why?"

"I thought it might be a good idea to turn it into a classroom and a playroom for the girls," she said, loading mashed potatoes onto her fork.

"Oh yes, Daddy!" Cassia and Alyssa agreed.

"How did you find it?" he asked. "I thought it had fallen down by now."

"Oh, please, Daddy!" the girls said. "It's a hidey house."

Regarding his daughters, Max smiled, and with a little more of their pleading, he was forced to allow it. They clapped and cheered with delight.

"Let me at least get a handyman in to make sure the roof and floor are still solid, first," Max said with a laugh. "No one has been in there in ages." He turned his attention to pouring more gravy on his potatoes.

As he did, the twins shot Susan worried looks, halting in their constant pushing of peas around their plates. Aha! Susan thought. So, they weren't allowed to play in the house. Winning their trust was important, and so she didn't mention seeing their toys in the place.

"It just seems like a waste to leave it not doing anything when it would serve so well," Susan said instead, and watched the girls visibly relax.

Max's smile was an odd one, half surprised and half appreciative. "Good thinking," he said. "I like your initiative."

"Thank you," she said.

It was ridiculous, but this little bit of praise from Max meant a lot to her. She found she wanted to do more to earn it again. And how silly was that? Ralph Waldo Emerson would be horrified at her. After all, in his essay titled *Self-Reliance,* he wrote how people should avoid conformity and false consistency and follow their own path. And here she was, needing the approval of her new husband.

Perhaps this was simply an emotional byproduct of her recent upheaval. It was all so new; having someone smile and say, "Well done," might only be of such great value while she was finding her feet. What an interesting theory to test. She'd have to wait and see if this reaction persisted.

Max was talking. Susan blinked, coming out of her reverie.

"Pardon?" she asked. "I seem to have drifted off into my own head there."

Cassia and Alyssa laughed raucously.

"Now, girls," Max said sternly. "Don't laugh like that."

"Those laughs were better suited to goblins than ladies," Susan said with raised eyebrows and a smile.

The girls stuck out their tongues. "Ladies?" they said, pulling faces. "Yuck!"

"Oh of course. I forgot it's fashionable now to be gargoyles."

Max sighed. "Please, Susan. We can't encourage such behavior. They must learn their manners."

Chastised, even gently, Susan drew her lips into a straight line and nodded. "Of course, you're right. Girls, I think you're done with dinner. Head upstairs to wash before bed."

"Aw!" they cried.

"Girls!" their father said sharply. "Go!"

They left the table with long faces. When they were gone, Max turned to Susan.

"You will have to be firmer with them. They are willful and unruly."

"Of course they are," Susan said. "I just don't want to make enemies of them so soon. I've found that things go smoother when children trust you and feel comfortable. I think things will go wrong if I rush in like an angry bull and order them around."

"You are the adult!" he said sharply. "You shouldn't be acting like their friend. Where is the discipline?"

"Yes, I am the adult. But I am a stranger to them. If we want this crazy relationship to stand even a snowball's chance, then I have to tread carefully, or by the time they're teenage girls, we will have no end of trouble! And I would like to remind you that you dropped them into my lap with no warning! So, if I'm taking longer than a day to achieve whatever you think I should be achieving, then—" Susan said.

"But you agreed," he said. "You said you would get them in hand."

Susan's breath came in quick pants as she tried to calm down. Fighting was probably the last thing they needed. "I agreed to teach them and look after them, and this is how I do it! So, you can either let me get on with it, or you can go and find yourself another sucker to saddle with them!"

She glared at him, angry that after one day with them, he was judging her. Didn't he know it was going to take time to fix all that was wrong? She had hardly gotten to know the girls! It was unfair and unrealistic of him to assume she would make more headway than she had.

"Well, I suppose I must let you do as you see fit," he said. "But they must be reined in."

"They will be," Susan said. "Now, what did you want to say before?"

"Only that I will be working until lunch tomorrow, with it being Saturday. You might want to make arrangements with Mrs. Potts for Sunday lunch, unless you'd like to cook," Max said. "She has Saturday afternoons and Sundays off."

"Good to know," Susan said. "I'll make arrangements. My cooking leaves much to be desired. In fact, my sisters all took turns cooking at home but made sure I never got one because the offerings were so awful."

She had expected him to smile or laugh. For the tension to break. The look of distaste that she got was surprising. "I mentioned it in the letters."

"I thought you were joking," Max said. "You know, playing down your skill."

"I don't do that," Susan said. "I call a spade a spade and a gargoyle a gargoyle."

They stared at each other over the table, and neither expression was pleasant. Susan sighed and laid her knife and fork on her plate. She picked up the girls' plates and took them through to the kitchen. This was turning out to be a difficult adjustment. Hopefully, things would get easier.

SUSAN'S TRUTH

The girls were clean and ready for their story, and Susan wished them good night before leaving them with their father to read a story. She went back downstairs and decided to clean up the kitchen. As she washed the dishes, she heard them reciting their bedtime prayers and couldn't help but harrumph. Honestly, he'd be better off teaching them to think their way out of problems.

As she packed the dishes away, Susan sighed, and the anger drained out of her. It was a trying time for them all, and she and Max were trying to do the impossible. Building a relationship with each other while she was trying to teach and build a relationship with the children. It was a lot of pressure.

Emily would suggest she pray about it. For a moment, Susan considered it, but only for a moment. Praying hadn't worked when she'd spent every night on her knees, begging for her parents to recover from the influenza that eventually took them. Why would prayer work now?

She stared around the kitchen, and it looked good and clean. At least she was good at that household duty. If she thought about it, she could probably learn to cook. How hard could it be? Perhaps she and the girls could learn from Mrs. Potts. It might be a good way to get them to learn about quantities and measurements. Perhaps they could bake bread or cookies, something fun. She'd have to speak to Mrs. Potts about it.

With nothing left to do in the kitchen, and her temper finally back under her control, Susan decided to speak to Max again. They couldn't afford to go to their separate beds angry.

He was in the dining room, reading his paper. When she came through, he put it down and, standing, took her hands in his.

"I can't help but feel awful that we had a disagreement," he said. "I'm sorry. I haven't had a woman in my life and my house like this since *she* left."

He looked so sincerely upset that Susan found her heart softening.

"I think fights were inevitable," she said. "We hardly know each other and are trying to raise two girls together. It's not going to be easy. But I am willing to try."

"Me too," he said.

She smiled. "Perhaps we can agree to give each other support and space as we need it? And I will learn to cook," she said.

"I didn't mean..." he said, looking deeply into her eyes. "I think you're remarkable as you are."

Heat hit her cheeks, and Susan found herself smiling like a dizzy schoolgirl. "You're quite remarkable too."

He smiled, and Susan's heart skipped several beats. There was something in that smile that acted like a magnet to her. She wanted to see it all the time, and surprisingly, she wanted to kiss the lips it lived on.

She'd never felt like that before and wasn't sure what to do. So, she squeezed his hands and smiled in return.

They could have stood like that all night, except Bunny appeared in the doorway and barked.

"Oh, Bunny!" Susan said, turning. "Come on, I have your dinner waiting in the kitchen." She went through with the dog yapping at her feet.

When she'd put the plate of chicken scraps and vegetables down for Bunny, who gobbled it up with delight, she went through and bid Max good night. He kissed her cheek as chastely as he had in the church, and she went upstairs. Had there been more in that kiss? Susan wondered, although she couldn't have said why.

As she opened Kierkegaard, snuggled in bed, she found her concentration lagging. Max kept popping up in her thoughts. Silly fantasies about kissing and holding him and what it would be like to wake up next to him. How juvenile. Anyone would think she was sixteen, the way she was behaving.

She blew out the candle and decided to try to sleep. Before she did, though, a quiet prayer slipped from her almost before she knew it was happening. Susan lay in the darkness and stared at the ceiling. Yes, she was angry at God for the death of her father. But that didn't mean she wasn't grateful for the gift of this new family.

CHAPTER 7

THE NEXT DAY, MAX WENT OFF TO WORK, AND Susan and the girls spent the morning clearing the path to the cabin. And just in time, too, because before the morning was done, a young man with a ladder appeared at the door saying Max had asked him to come and do repairs on the cabin roof.

Susan led him around the house and watched as he climbed the ladder and inspected the roof. There were a few tiles loose, and while he fixed them, Susan and the girls set about cleaning the inside.

The girls lost interest quickly and chose to play outside, but that was fine. It was Saturday, and they were still little. With the room clear, Susan had an idea.

"Come on, girls, let's go to the trader," she said.

They whooped and smiled, leaving the mud pies they'd been making in the soft ground.

"Go and wash up at the outside pump," Susan said with a laugh, noting their very muddy hands.

When they were presentable, she left Mrs. Potts keeping an eye on the handyman and off they went.

They took a brisk walk in the cold under a bright blue sky. It was only four blocks to the store, and the girls had boundless energy, skipping and laughing as they went. When they reached the trader, Susan pushed the door open to the jingle of bells and let the girls go in first. They made a beeline for the sweets jars up on the counter.

"Can we have some?" they begged.

"Only if you behave like little ladies while we're in this store," Susan said. "Can you do that?"

The girls exchanged looks and nodded. With their noses in the air, they minced around the store, trying to act like princesses.

Susan bought a large chalkboard and two smaller slates for the classroom. She also invested in colored chalks, a box of paints, some paper and pencils, erasers, and dusters. That should do for a start. Since she was putting it all on Max's tab, she didn't want to go too wild.

"Are you opening a school?" the old lady behind the counter asked. She had her hair up in a bun and bright smiling eyes.

"Of sorts," Susan said. "I'm teaching these two princesses."

"Are you their new governess?" the woman asked pleasantly as she wrote down the purchases.

"Oh, actually I'm Mr. Peterson's new wife," Susan said.

The old lady looked up, surprised.

Alyssa chose that moment to make a most awfully rude noise with her mouth. Susan turned and gave her a warning look.

"Oh?" the old lady said, eyeing her and Alyssa. "We've all been wondering if he would try married life again. It was such a tragic story, her running out like that. But of course, you know all about it, don't you?"

Susan knew about it. Whether it was everything, she wasn't sure.

It was Cassia's turn to be rude, making a windy noise similar to the one her sister had made.

"Well, I'm sure everything will be fine," the woman said, looking put out by the girls' behavior. "You certainly have your work cut out for you."

The girls refused to stop making that infernal noise. They just kept on and on.

"Honestly, girls!" Susan said, rounding on them. "Please!"

"We're not listening to you," Alyssa said. "You're not our mother."

Susan sighed. "You're right. But that's no reason for us to forget our manners. Or don't you remember what your father said last night at dinner?"

After a moment, the girls calmed down, and with Cassia's thumb back in her mouth and their heads down, they apologized to the lady, who took it graciously.

With the prices tallied and added to Max's tab, it was time to go.

"I'll get the goods delivered this afternoon," the old lady said.

"Thank you," Susan said, and added a bag of boiled sweets to the purchase for the girls. Perhaps she could use them as rewards so she could have some peace.

On the way home, they each sucked a sweet, and the walk went by in relative silence. As they walked, Susan noticed that the girls always held hands wherever they went. They were never far from each other. Susan thought that odd, or perhaps it was a twin thing.

When they reached the house, they found the handyman on his way out.

"All done, Mrs. Peterson," he said. "The roof and floor are fine. It's a well-built cabin."

"Thank you," she said.

It was time for lunch, which Mrs. Potts had made for them. "There are ham and cheese sandwiches for now, and a cheese and onion pie in the cold room for tonight. For tomorrow's lunch, roast chicken with vegetables. Just put it in the oven to warm. You can manage that, right?"

"I think so," Susan said. "Although cooking lessons would be good too, sometime?"

Mrs. Potts beamed and nodded. "We'll work something out. Good luck," she said, and with a pat on the head for each child, she disappeared through the kitchen door.

Having Mrs. Potts at the house with her had been reassuring, and Susan didn't realize just how much she'd been relying on the housekeeper to be an extra set of eyes and hands until she was gone. There was a whole afternoon ahead of her, and she didn't know what to do with the girls.

They ate together at the kitchen table. With blatant disregard for how much food cost, the girls pulled the ham out of their sandwiches and gave it to Bunny, who snapped it up. Coming from a household where each meal was a blessing, this rubbed Susan the wrong way completely. She snapped at them, and with great reluctance, the girls stopped feeding the dog.

After lunch, it was nap time.

"Come on, let's go and have a nap," Susan said, finding her patience beginning to wane. Any more from them and she might start screaming. It had been a trying day so far.

"No," Alyssa said. "Don't want to."

"Me either," Cassia said. They stuck their chins out like they had at the store.

"Come on," Susan said. "You know it's nap time. Please don't fight with me."

The twins pursed their lips, folded their arms, and refused to budge. Susan tried to be nice one last time, but they shot her down again, refusing to move. All right. They were testing boundaries. She had expected that.

"Get upstairs and have your nap now!" she roared, pointing to the stairs, her other hand on her hip. Just like Mother used to do.

It didn't work. The girls gripped their chairs and refused to let go. Susan tried to pull them off, but as she got one girl up and tried to grab the other, the first one would sit back down again and refuse to move. She was losing her cool.

Susan had never agreed with hitting children. She found it distasteful. However, in the past she'd been able to go to the children's parents for help with their unruly offspring.

She was supposed to be the parent now. It was all up to her. She had to get things under control With a grunt, she wrenched Cassia up from her chair. As the child's bottom came into view, without thinking, Susan used the flat of her hand to smack it.

Cassia let out a scream and grabbed her bottom, tears streaming down her face. Susan didn't think she'd hit her that hard. Her hand wasn't even stinging, and yet the child cried as though she'd tried to murder her.

Alyssa was up off her chair and in her twin's arms in seconds. They huddled together, shooting Susan rotten looks.

The shock of it all immobilized Susan for a moment, and then her temper flared. How dare they behave like this? Grabbing them both by the arm, she dragged them upstairs and into their room.

"Now! You will lie down and go to sleep!" she yelled. "Do you hear me?"

The girls, their faces white and tearstained, nodded and climbed into their beds, pulling the covers right over their heads. Susan was panting like a winded rhinoceros as she closed their door and ran to her room.

Once inside, she sank onto her bed in shock. She'd never hit anyone before. Never. How had things fallen apart like that? What would Max say when he came home? Would they fight again?

She curled up into a ball and closed her eyes. There had to be some way to deal with this, but she couldn't think what that could be. How could she make this right? Susan didn't know, and she found emotion overriding her logic. She was sad and lost and alone. She wasn't a mother. She wasn't even a good governess. Clearly, she shouldn't be anywhere near children. What kind of sick joke was fate playing on her?

She'd have to tell Max she couldn't do this. Seeing the look of horror and shock on Cassia's sweet little face as her hand acted on its own…it wouldn't leave her. Susan hugged her pillow, shoved her face in it, and cried until she drifted off into an exhausted sleep.

When she woke, she rolled over and stared at her bedside table. For a moment she couldn't figure out what was missing, but the fact that something was registered immediately.

Her watch was there, her stub of a candle in a candle holder, her jar of hand cream she put on before bed each night. They were all there. What wasn't was her book.

Susan sat up, ice sliding through her veins. Her precious book. Oh no! Kierkegaard!

CHAPTER 8

With leaden limbs, Susan made her way out of her room. She checked in with the girls, only to find their beds rumpled but no sign of them anywhere. That was disturbing. What if they had run out of the house? What if something horrible had happened to them while she was crying and being stupid?

Panic began to rise in her chest like stinging bile. Where were the girls?

She checked the kitchen, the parlor, and their father's study. He kept the door closed but not locked. They were not there. She tried the cupboard under the stairs and found it only full of mops, brooms, and dusters.

All right, where else could they be? Where else would the girls go?

She went into the yard and found Bunny sniffing a bush. After some inspection, it became clear the dog was hunting mice and not at all perturbed that the girls were in fact missing.

And then an idea came to Susan. Why hadn't she thought of this first? Of course they would run there. It was their little hidey house.

She went down the path to the cabin and flung the door open. Sitting in the middle of the floor, a pen and a bottle of ink each in hand, no doubt pilfered from their father's office, sat the girls. Their dark hair hung over their faces, and they were drawing with glee on something.

As Susan stepped into the room, they squealed in surprise and both shot to their feet. Alyssa knocked her ink bottle over, and it spilled on the floor, running into the wood grain and all over the thing they were drawing on.

"There you are. I was so worried!" Susan said as she rushed over to the ink bottle to turn it right-side up. It was only as she bent to retrieve the bottle that she noticed what the girls had been drawing on, and her heart stopped.

Blinking back rapidly forming tears, Susan stared at the thing now drenched in black ink on the floor. Her mouth worked and no sound came out. Her mind was a horrific, startled blank. It was her book. Her father's book, and it was ruined.

"We're sorry!" Alyssa cried, backing to the wall with her hands over her bottom. "We're sorry!"

Cassia followed her sister, whimpering as Susan gently picked up her book. She tried to hold back her sobs and couldn't. It was too much. This was her father's book, and now another piece of him was gone. She wasn't even angry, just deeply wounded as though the girls had stabbed her with a knife.

The door opened, and a shadow fell across her.

"Ah! Here you all are," Max said. His tone was bright, but it changed in an instant. "What's going on?"

The girls rushed to him, babbling, but Susan said nothing. She turned to him with her book clutched to her chest. Their gazes met for only an instant. Something must have passed from her to him because his expression grew grave, and he cast an angry eye on his daughters.

"What have you done?" he asked.

THEY SAT AT THE KITCHEN TABLE, SUSAN clutching a mug of chamomile tea Max had made her. She sipped it while Alyssa and Cassia tried to explain. Being small, they were no good at clearly expressing themselves verbally, but they were trying.

Susan had made them angry, and they wanted to let her know. That was the gist of it. Then it was Susan's turn to explain the morning in detail, which she did. Max listened to everything, and when it was all done, he sighed and rubbed his hands over his face.

It was only then that Susan saw how tired he looked. His day had been long as well, and his week a trying one. This wasn't helping him. Once again, she felt a prayer slip from her, unbidden.

Please help me do better, Lord.

"All right. I know what's going on here. It's not the first time we've had this, is it?" he asked his daughters.

They shook their heads.

"This has happened every time you've had a new nanny, hasn't it?" he asked.

Again, they nodded.

"We don't want another nanny," Cassia said around her thumb, which hadn't left her mouth since Susan found them in the cabin.

"I understand that," Max said, his tone terse. "But you need to understand that Susan isn't another nanny. I have married her. She is my wife now, and she is going to be a mother to you. Eventually..." he held up his hands at the children's protest. "She isn't going anywhere. She won't leave. I suggest you get used to that idea."

The girls sulked and stared at the tabletop.

"And you owe her an apology," he said. "You see, this book was Susan's daddy's book, and it reminded her of him. Now since you poured my ink all over it, you've taken that piece of her daddy away from her."

Cassia began to wail. She dropped her head on the table and cried.

Max drew her into his arms and held her. "There, there. We can try to make things right, but I need you two to be nice. Susan is trying her best. I need you two to try. Can you do that?"

After a long hesitation, they nodded.

"Good. Now you will be spending the evening in your room. I will bring you dinner, and you can come out of your room tomorrow. Do you understand?"

The girls nodded, and when he released them, they trooped upstairs without a word, once again holding hands.

"I'm sorry about the book," Max said. "I'll order another. I know it won't be the same, but..."

"Thank you," Susan said, recognizing the olive branch that this offer was. "I'm sorry about the girls. I thought they were napping."

He sighed and took her hand. "They are sneaky little devils when they want to be. But I thank God for them every day. And for you. Please, just give us some time. You'll see we're not a bad family to be part of."

Susan smiled despite her tears and sniffed a laugh.

"That's better," Max said. "I'm sorry I'm so late. There was a meeting at the bank after hours. Mr. Morgan hates taking up trading time to have a word with the staff, so it was this afternoon or never."

Just then there was a knock at the door, and Bunny, who had been sleeping on the hall rug, burst into angry barks.

Max rose and went to the door while Susan dried her eyes on her handkerchief.

"Ah, Susan..."

She stood and came through to the hall, where several parcels were blocking the doorway along with a tubby man with flaming red hair.

"What's all this?" Max asked her.

Susan had completely forgotten about the things she'd bought from the store. "Oh, I bought a few things at the trader for the classroom. I hope you don't mind."

Max inspected the purchases and signed the account. "I can see why you need them," he said. "Bill, can you help me take this all around to the cabin out back?"

The red-haired man called Bill nodded, and they took the goods around. Susan followed and had them mount the chalkboard on the wall. Things were looking good.

"Perhaps if the girls are constructively occupied, they will have less time for mischief," Max said.

"That's what I'm hoping," Susan said.

With Max's help, Susan spent a few hours getting the room set up for school the coming Monday. They had chairs and a table piled in the back room, which they hauled out and cleaned. There was an old rug that just needed sweeping and made a good floor cover, and a bookcase to hold the children's books. Susan found an old wicker basket to put the dolls, blocks, and other toys in, and suddenly the room looked like a classroom.

Working with Max was fun. He was strong, clever, and not at all averse to rolling up his sleeves and getting mucky. Susan appreciated the support he was giving her, and so, when he mentioned that in the morning, they would all be heading off to church, she didn't refuse.

With the classroom mostly done, they went back inside the house to find the girls sitting in the kitchen, helping themselves to glasses of milk.

"Thirsty," Cassia said by way of explanation. She was generally a child of few words.

"That's all right," Max said. "Are you ready to be my good little angels?"

They nodded.

"All right, then you may eat dinner with us at the table," Max said.

The girls smiled, and once Susan figured out how to warm up dinner, they ate with no drama at all. After dinner, the girls went upstairs, washed, and got into bed with no fuss. It was as though little switches had been flipped in their brains, and suddenly, they were different people.

Susan knew it wouldn't last. Nothing was ever that easy. She was grateful for this respite, though, and went to bed feeling if not happy, then at least more at ease.

CHAPTER 9

The clouds came out of nowhere, it seemed, and the Peterson family woke to a white world, dusted with snow. Alyssa and Cassia were thrilled and could hardly sit still long enough for Susan to tie pretty yellow ribbons in their long dark hair.

She made toast and jam for breakfast since anything else would require actual cooking, and it went down rather well. With everyone fed they went out to the stable, where Roger had the cart and Rainbow ready for them.

Max helped his daughters into the back and then helped Susan onto the seat up front next to him. He smiled. "You look lovely."

"Oh, thank you," Susan said. She was dressed in a navy-blue wool dress with her gray coat and a blue scarf and hat. It was her best winter dress, and she saved it for special occasions. It was pleasing to hear Max compliment her. After a slight hesitation, she said, "You look dashing yourself."

He did. In a dark gray suit that brought out the deep blue of his eyes, with his hair combed back, he was the picture of a fine gentleman.

"Well, here we are," Max said with a smile a little while later. He jumped down and helped Susan down as well. He went to help the girls.

Susan took in the scene around her. The churchyard was full of people arriving in carts, buggies, and carriages. Some walked, and others rode horses. There were several young boys seeing to the horses as people went to the church doors, which stood wide open.

"You are here!"

It was Emily. Susan turned and hugged her sister, who had snuck up on her.

"I told Sadie you would be," Emily said, beaming. She was a vision in a peach scarf and hat. "Morning, Max, girls."

They greeted her as Sadie, Kyle, and Tony came up from where they'd left their cart.

Sadie embraced Susan and smiled. "How are you holding up?"

"Fine," Susan said.

Sadie studied her face with a frown and then took her arm. "We should get inside. Our dear minister is a stickler for punctuality."

The pews were filling up, and they only managed to find a row with enough space for them all at the back of the church. This suited Susan just fine, and she prepared herself to be bored for an hour or so. Sitting so close next to Max, smelling his cologne, stirred things in her she was certain were inappropriate for church.

When the service started, Alyssa and Cassia soon became bored and started fidgeting. They weren't the only ones. It seemed all the small children in the congregation, and there were quite a few, could only stand having to sit still for about twenty minutes, and then they couldn't help but move.

The minister took it all in his stride and had them stand to sing several hymns, which the children seemed to enjoy.

Then it was time for the reading, and Susan watched the children either jiggle like they needed to go to the bathroom or fall asleep on their parents' laps. Alyssa and Cassia seemed to turn off and, holding hands, they stared into space, not blinking or moving. It was as though they were lifelike statues.

"The reading today is from Philippians 4:11-13: 'Not that I am speaking of being in need, for I have learned in whatever situation I am to be content. I know how to be brought low, and I know how to abound. In any and every circumstance, I have learned the secret of facing plenty and hunger, abundance and need. I can do all things through him who strengthens me.'"

The minister looked out over the congregation and smiled. "We've had hard times lately. Some of us more than others. We must remember that the good Lord is always there for us. All we need to do is ask for His help. And if we have not been brought low at this time, then it might be God's will that we act as angels to our neighbors and help them, showing the compassion of Christ.

"We know this from Proverbs 28:27: 'Whoever gives to the poor will not want, but he who hides his eyes will get many a curse.' Bear this in mind as we go forth into this new year, and let's be the community that stands together and prospers."

Susan listened and felt unusually touched by the sermon. It hit home far more than many had in past years.

When the service was done, Max invited Susan's sisters and their husbands back to the house for coffee.

"I'm sure Susan has missed you both terribly," he said.

Amazed at his astuteness, Susan nodded. "I have."

"Well, we'd be delighted, wouldn't we?" Emily asked, eyeing everyone in such a way that their disagreement was unthinkable.

They rode to the house and soon were ensconced in the kitchen, with Susan putting a large pot of coffee on to boil.

"It's about the only thing we would let you make at home," Emily said with a laugh. "Her coffee is great; everything else is…"

"Horrible," Sadie said. "Well, it's true. Sadly, Susan spent all her time with Father and none with the cook. Back in the days when we had one."

Susan sighed. "Are you quite done making fun of me?"

Her sisters shrugged and laughed. "Sorry, dear," Emily said. "We do love you."

"How is married life?" Kyle asked Max. "You surviving?"

Max smiled and nodded. "Yeah, we're doing all right. We've had a few hiccups, but I think we're fine now."

"Brave last words," Tony said.

Susan found a tin of Mrs. Potts' cookies in the pantry and laid them on a plate for all to have.

Alyssa and Cassia, looking bored with the adult conversation, pleaded to be allowed to go and play outside in the snow.

"All right," Susan said. "But take your milk and cookies with you and put them up on the porch railing so Bunny doesn't get them."

The girls laughed, and Cassia gave her a hug around her thighs before walking out, carefully holding her plate and mug. The gesture almost brought Susan to tears. She'd been petrified the little girl would hate her for what she'd done, but she seemed to have forgotten about it.

With the children taken care of and her sisters pouring the coffee as though they lived here, Susan took a seat next to Max.

"That was an interesting sermon," she said. "Was it because of the sick sheep?"

Tony laughed. "Emily, you never said your sister was a detective."

"She's not, but she is very smart. Nothing gets by our Sue," she said with a proud grin.

"You're right," Kyle said. "Bear Creek has had a host of issues lately. We've had cattle and sheep stolen, others getting mysteriously sick, farmers going belly up and losing their land..."

"And there were all those fires at the end of summer," Sadie said.

"Yeah, and those. Just a run of extremely bad luck," Kyle said.

Susan frowned. "Is it normal to have this much?"

"I've never known it, have you, Max?" Tony asked.

Max shook his head. "No. But there is a first time for everything."

CHAPTER 10

Susan had plenty to keep her occupied for the next couple of weeks. Alyssa and Cassia were resistant to her officially teaching them anything. However, if she turned the lessons into games and competitions with sweets as rewards, the little girls were quick to get onboard.

When not in lessons, the girls would still fight with her about things like washing up, getting dressed, and tidying their room. These were all character-building exercises, and Susan insisted they do them.

After some trial and error, she made them a chart, which they stuck on their door. Each day they could move the pictures that represented the various activities to the side that said "completed." Somehow this visual aid worked, and knowing what to expect each day, the girls cooperated with less fuss.

What they enjoyed most were Mrs. Potts' cooking lessons, because there was always something yummy to eat when they were finished. She taught the girls and Susan two days a week, and so far Susan had learned to make bread, stew, and an omelet.

To get the girls out of the house, Susan took them to the farm a couple of times. It was pleasant to sit with her sisters while the girls ran about with the sheep and the dogs. It was just about her only adult conversation.

Max was snowed under at work. The bank in Crystal Lake had been robbed, and now the mine workers in the area had to come to Bear Creek to get their money. He assured Susan that in the new month, things would calm down. Once everyone got used to the new workload. But for now, he came home just in time for dinner most days. Even though she saw little of him, the time they spent together made her feel they were getting closer. They talked about everything, sitting in the parlor at night, watching the fire burn down low. He was a most open-minded man and wanted his girls to learn and explore the world. Susan was pleased. Especially since she had no intention of teaching them embroidery and deportment.

With February coming closer, all conversation with Emily turned to Valentine's Day. She was a fanatic about it. The local White Swan Hotel was having a dinner and dance that night, and Emily had decided both her sisters and their husbands would have to attend. She'd even gone so far as to book tables for them.

Truthfully, Susan liked the idea of Max to herself for an evening. It would hopefully bring them closer together. She found she had a high regard for him and missed him when he wasn't around. This was unusual, and Susan wasn't sure what to make of it. But he was handsome, attentive, and bright. She couldn't ask for more. And on his part, Max seemed taken with her. She caught him staring at her with a strange look on his face that made her heart skip several beats.

Could it be this business arrangement was growing into something else entirely? She would never say it out loud, but Susan fervently hoped so.

February brought with it a whole new attitude in the town. As the weather grew warmer and all about, the wildflowers began to bloom, everyone's minds filled with thoughts of spring and what that would mean.

On the farm, the ewes started giving birth to tiny little lambs that wobbled and tumbled on their long spindly legs. Alyssa and Cassia were enthralled with the little creatures, and Susan brought them over to see the wonder of new life almost every day.

Cassia had come around. She liked Susan, and often they would read books together with the little girl leaning on Susan's shoulder or sitting in her lap and helping her turn the pages. She loved to color and had a real flair for drawing. Her ability to copy shapes and put them together to make pictures was quite remarkable.

Alyssa was not as keen on Susan. She still seemed determined to fight to the death, and it was wearing Susan down. No matter what Susan did, Alyssa would be ungrateful and hostile. It was becoming too much for Susan, and she found herself on her knees one night in her room, with her hands clasped before her, contemplating asking God for help. That was how desperate she was. Of course, now she felt like a hypocrite. How could she ask for help when she'd been angry with Him for so long?

But desperation was a powerful motivator, and after a particularly trying day, Susan found herself asking for guidance, not for her own peace of mind, but for

Alyssa. The little girl was spinning out of control, and it wasn't good for her.

"Please, for Alyssa's sake. Help me, Lord," she said.

She wasn't sure if God had even heard her. It would be nice to get a note saying, "The Creator has heard you. Leave it with us." But no such luck.

So, she crawled into bed, hugged her pillow, and fell asleep.

THE NEXT DAY STARTED OFF AS USUAL, WITH SUSAN fighting to get Alyssa out of bed. Then while Mrs. Potts gave Cassia her breakfast, Susan fought with Alyssa to get dressed. And then she fought with the child to get some food into her, and so the day progressed. By the time it was lunch, Susan was more than ready to snap.

It seemed Mrs. Potts was feeling something similar, and she sat Susan down with a cup of tea while the children were sleeping and had a chat with her.

"You're fighting a losing battle with that one," she said. "She's got the stubbornness of the Irish. And I'd know. My mother was Irish, and there was no telling that woman what to do. Ever."

"Oh," Susan said.

"So, you know what I used to do to get her to play along?" Mrs. Potts asked.

Susan shook her head.

"I'd lay it all out for my mother. I'd tell her what needed to be done and what would happen if she didn't do it. And then I'd leave her," Mrs. Potts said. She took a sip of her tea.

"And then what happened?" Susan asked, intrigued.

Mrs. Potts smiled. "She'd do it. Whatever it was. Sometimes I'd make it sound like it was all her idea, and then she couldn't wait to get it done. Funny, isn't it? I remember telling her that she needed to see the doctor and then waiting a day or two for her to tell me to call the doctor in. It was uncanny how well that worked."

"That's a very interesting approach," Susan said. "I don't know if we can wait a few days for Alyssa to brush her teeth or put on clean clothes. But I suppose I could try it. Yes, I think that might be worth a try. You're a genius, Mrs. Potts."

Mrs. Potts' full cheeks turned a delicate pink. "Well, you know. It's just some advice; take it or leave it."

"Oh, I'll take it," Susan said and, smiling, she went upstairs to think.

By the end of nap time, Susan had a plan for dealing with Alyssa. Since anything Susan suggested was instantly knocked down, she decided to let Alyssa come up with ideas. Should she fail, Susan would have a suggestion all ready.

At first Alyssa was as hostile as ever, until she began to see that she could suggest things. If she did and they were possible to do, Susan would agree. This seemed to make Alyssa cooperative. For the next few days, she tried out various versions of that strategy, and some worked while others didn't.

A week went by, and the fights became less frequent and less severe. Alyssa seemed to follow Cassia's example more often and let Susan cuddle her and read to her. There was still a long way to go, but she was making headway, and Susan was thrilled.

Her progress didn't go unnoticed.

"The girls seemed very contented today," Max said one day after dinner.

They were having their time together in the parlor. Susan sat with him on the sofa. He put his arm around her shoulders, and she let her head rest on his shoulder. It was lovely to sit like that.

"I think we've found a method of working together where we don't have to fight," Susan said.

"That's a relief," Max said. He smiled. "You truly are amazing. The effort you put into understanding our girls is nothing short of miraculous. I'm certain there isn't another woman alive who would spend this much time and effort on them."

"Oh, I don't know," Susan said. "There are a lot of really dedicated teachers out there."

"But you're more than a teacher," Max said. "Cassia is already calling you 'mother' to Mrs. Potts. Oh, that's a secret, by the way. Mrs. Potts wasn't supposed to tell me, but she thought it was so sweet when Cassia told her."

Susan felt her breath catch in her throat. Cassia thought of her as a mother? It was amazing. Things were really coming together. She smiled at Max. "Well, I wasn't expecting that," she said.

"Why not?" he asked. "You're the closest thing the girls have had to a mother their whole lives. Others have looked after them, but no one has ever tried to connect with them like you have. I'm proud of you."

Susan chuckled nervously. "This conversation is turning odd."

"Is it?" he asked. "You know I spend so much time talking to people about their finances and their future prospects that I don't even know what normal conversation is anymore."

"Well, I speak to kids every day, so..." Susan shrugged, and Max laughed.

"Quite the pair, aren't we?" he asked.

Susan nodded. "I like who we are."

Max nodded, and as his head bent toward hers, Susan found she couldn't wait any longer. She tilted her face up and met his lips with a kiss. Max reacted in surprise and then suddenly he was kissing her, drawing her to him with urgency and heart-pounding passion. Susan hadn't expected that, and yet she found it perfectly appropriate. They were married, after all.

Susan felt herself being swept up on a tide of something she didn't dare give a name to, and before she knew what was happening, she and Max were quite intertwined around each other.

Perhaps he realized where this was heading because Max pulled away from her a little. "Susan," he said.

Oh no, he's going to stop, she thought.

All the longing looks, the touching hands, the almost-kisses. She couldn't go back to that. There was just no way.

Susan reached up and ran her fingers through his hair.

"Are you sure? I don't want to scare you off," he said.

She smiled and shook her head, reaching her lips up to his. From the moment they touched again, she was swept away.

CHAPTER 11

February 14 dawned. The sky was a deep blue; the sun shone brightly, and the day was warm and mild. There was a gentle breeze, blowing scents of the newly bloomed flowers across Bear Creek, when Susan woke.

It was a Tuesday. She needed to teach the girls their lessons before they would go to the Valentine's Day picnic at the church, and she would get ready for her dinner with Max.

Mrs. Potts had agreed to take the girls to the church Valentine's Day picnic and then look after them until Susan and Max returned home.

Susan hurried to dress before going downstairs for breakfast. She and Max could hardly keep their hands off each other and sat so their feet could meet under the table. Susan felt giddy. Was this love?

Max went off to work. As he left, he kissed her cheek. "You'll be here when I get home?"

"Of course," she said.

He nodded, looking oddly nervous, and walked down the path and out the gate. What was that about?

Susan didn't have time to worry, though; she had lessons to get through. The girls made paper hearts and flowers and cut them out, stringing them all over the classroom. It was Cassia's idea to make friendship cards for all their friends at church who would be at the picnic.

They had lunch, and the girls had a brief nap before it was time to get them dressed in their best yellow dresses with ribbons in their hair. As they left the house, holding Mrs. Potts' hands, Susan smiled and waved. They looked so happy.

Now she had to get ready for a romantic evening out with the man she loved.

Susan went out to the wash house, carting buckets of hot water from the kitchen cauldron to the metal tub. When there was enough water, she got in and soaped herself up and washed her body and hair until she was squeaky clean.

Back in the kitchen she refilled the cauldron with water from the pump, in case Max wanted a wash.

Next, she went upstairs and began the arduous task of styling and drying her hair. That took ages. She had planned an elaborate updo with ringlets, but since her hair was notoriously resistant to curling, Susan went with a simpler style consisting of a bun on her head with several braids wrapped around it. The effect was neat and comfortable. Anyway, transforming completely into someone Max wouldn't even recognize when he arrived home was silly. She wanted him to like what she was wearing, not be shocked by it.

She had just finished applying what makeup she had when she heard the front door close and Max's voice calling up the stairs.

"Hello!" he called. "Are you there, Susan?"

"I'm here!" she called.

Perhaps he didn't hear her because she heard his voice take on a more panicked tone as he called her name again.

"Max!" she called.

She heard him coming up the stairs and, only in her gown, she went to open the door.

Max looked flustered. "Oh, there you are. Didn't you hear me calling?"

"I did, and I answered," Susan said. "Are you all right?"

He sighed and shook his head. "I know it's stupid, but I keep thinking I'll come home and find you gone." He drew her to him and kissed her. "I couldn't live through that."

Susan's heart beat far too fast, and her body responded to his touch as it had the night before. But this was no time. She kissed his cheek and gently pushed him back. "I'm not going anywhere," she said. "Except out to a fancy dinner with my husband. So, get ready, or we'll be late, and Emily will string us both up."

He recovered and, smiling, asked, "Is there some hot water in the kitchen? I'd love to wash up."

"Yes, there's a cauldron full," she said.

He nodded. "I'll get to it then."

She closed the door and heard him go downstairs. It was exciting. This would be their first outing as husband and wife.

Climbing into her blue dress, which showed off her shoulders, Susan was happy with the result. She looked neat, presentable, and appealing. The color brought out the green in her eyes, and her brown hair had a glossy look that was most fetching.

She was only sad she had no jewelry to wear. They'd had to sell all of Mother's jewels when she died, and there was never money for such luxuries. Oh well.

She stepped onto the landing and found Max ready. He was in his charcoal suit, looking very dapper.

"Before we go," he said. "I have a little something for you."

It was a small velvet box. Susan's hands shook a little as she took it and opened it. Inside was a string of perfect white pearls and earrings to match. She stared at Max, hardly able to breathe, let alone speak.

"They were my mother's," he said. "She was a fine woman, strong and brilliant, like you, in fact. That's why I thought you might like them."

"Oh, Max," Susan said. "They are beyond lovely. Your mother was a lucky woman."

"Indeed, she was," Max said. "Until the train derailment that took her and my father's lives. Don't worry; it was ages ago. I'm just glad I've found someone to give her pearls to."

Susan touched them gingerly. "I will treasure them."

He smiled. "I think every beautiful woman should have something beautiful to wear for special occasions."

He did the silver clasp for her as she slipped the earrings on, and her outfit was complete. Max sighed. "You are stunningly beautiful. I fear all the other men will try to take you away from me."

"Not a chance," Susan said, kissing his cheek. "I'm all yours."

Smiling, he drew her into a quick kiss, and her knees went weak. How did he have this effect on her? It was baffling.

This time when she whispered a prayer of thanks, it was more conscious.

The White Swan Hotel was lit by many lamps that evening, and there were roses and carnations aplenty decorating the entrance.

Susan and Max made their way through the lobby and into the dining room, where tables ringed an open area of floor. In that space a band was just warming up. Along the far wall, a set of long tables had been placed, and already there were covered dishes suspended over candles to keep the food warm. The air smelled of perfume, delicious food, and excitement.

Susan found her sisters and their husbands already seated at their table with glasses of wine in front of them. Sadie was lovely in red, and Emily was a vision in emerald green. They greeted each other, and then Susan and Max took their seats.

Most of Bear Creek had turned out for the dance. Max greeted several of his colleagues from the bank, including Mr. Morgan, who looked, to Susan, like a bulldog with sagging jowls.

As the evening commenced, the dishes' covers came off, and the air was filled with the most delicious smells. There was roast lamb and chicken, a thick beef stew with rice, baked potatoes, roasted vegetables, and loaves of crusty baked bread.

Susan and Max ate their fill, with Emily chastising Tony for the pile of food he put on his plate. Then came the dancing. It surprised Susan that Max was a very good dancer. He had great rhythm, and she found herself having the best time.

Next came dessert, which was more chocolate than Susan had ever seen. Chocolate truffles, chocolate cake, hot chocolate...you name it; it had chocolate in it. She had a little of almost everything before her stomach reached its limits, and she was forced to stop or be sick.

More dancing ensued to the lively band, and by the time the evening was over, Susan and Max were both sweaty and exhausted. Luckily, the ride home in the cart was quick.

They found the house quiet, the girls asleep, and Mrs. Potts all tucked up on the sofa.

"We mustn't wake them," Susan whispered as they made their way upstairs.

She took Max by the hand, and it was the most natural thing for them to fall into bed together as a married couple. The whole evening was a blessing, and Susan found herself offering another prayer of thanks to God for bringing her out to Bear Creek.

CHAPTER 12

Susan woke with the most delicious feeling in her belly. She rolled over to find Max lying next to her, watching her.

"You were watching me sleep?" she asked.

He nodded. "Get used to it."

"You're strange..." she smiled. "We should probably get dressed; the girls will be up soon."

Sliding out of bed, Susan hurried to her room, where she quickly pulled on a blouse and skirt.

It was another fine day and she felt elated.

Downstairs, she found Alyssa and Cassia having bowls of porridge that Mrs. Potts had made. The housekeeper was all smiles, and they were laughing about something that had happened at the picnic.

"Susan!" Cassia cried when she saw her. "Tommy Perkins fell in the duck pond!"

"On my goodness!" Susan said, making her eyes go theatrically wide.

"He did," Cassia said and giggled.

"The minister fished him out," Alyssa said.

Susan smiled as she sat down and accepted a bowl of porridge from the housekeeper. "Well, you'll have to tell me all about it."

Max came in and kissed the girls good morning before treating Susan to another kiss of her own. His hand lingered on her shoulder, and electricity shot through Susan. She was thrilled that her little family was coming together so nicely.

Breakfast done, Max went off to the bank, and the girls went to their lessons. To say that Susan was distracted was an understatement. She was not focused on lessons at all. All she could think of was Max. Being away from him was horrible. She wanted to find any excuse to see him. Maybe she could drop in on him for lunch.

"Girls, I need to go to the store," she said, just before lunchtime.

"Can we come?" they asked. "We'll be good!"

They looked so eager that Susan nodded. "All right. Let's take Mrs. Potts and go and buy some seeds to plant in our kitchen garden. What do you think of that?"

They cheered. Anything to get out of lessons. Anything to see Max. Susan could nip to the bank while Mrs. Potts had the girls in the store.

They were a happy party that walked to the store. The girls skipped, and Mrs. Potts read a list of seeds they should buy off a page in a magazine.

"Lettuce, cucumber, tomato, onions," she read. "And soon we must plant some summer squash as well."

Susan listened with less than half an ear. Max had somewhat consumed her world. As they walked along, she noticed a lot of men on horses in town. They were lined up outside the bank and apothecary. Some sat on their horses while others, laughing and joking, walked along to the store and the bathhouse.

Perhaps they were just moving through. They looked rough, like they'd been sleeping outdoors for a while.

Vagrants came through all towns, Susan was sure of it. One man with white-blond hair and dark eyes tipped his hat to her. She nodded and ushered the children past him in a hurry.

She didn't think the girls should be anywhere near a man like that.

Inside the store, she noted, there was a tall young man behind the counter today, and he looked tense as well. He nodded to them, keeping his eyes on the strangers.

They went to the shelf where the seeds were arranged in little brown paper bags with their names written on them. Susan read sweet potatoes, onions, cabbage, peppers, and so on printed on the labels. Cassia and Alyssa were full of suggestions of what to get.

Susan was finding it difficult to concentrate. After all, Max was just out there, and she wanted to see him more than anything. This was madness. So many philosophers throughout the ages had thought of love as a construct of the mind. How was she to know if this was the real thing? And why was it so imperative that she know? Surely, she still had her own unique identity and could survive on her own? Surely, things hadn't changed that much in a few short weeks?

Susan didn't know the answer, but she felt an undeniable tug, drawing her to Max at all hours of the day. Only when she was in his arms would the longing finally stop, and she could rest. How did people live like this?

"Mrs. Potts," Susan said. "I want to pop in to visit Max." She eyed the men who were still milling about outside. "Just to make sure everything is fine with us spending more money."

"I've got the girls," Mrs. Potts said. "I'll keep them at the seeds." She cast a furtive eye at the sweet jars on the counter.

Susan nodded and smiled. "Good."

She went out the front door of the store and trotted across to the bank. There was a cue of people waiting to see the tellers. Max was behind the counter, helping an old lady. He was counting out notes and coins for her one at a time.

Susan waited. While the line moved along, each person getting their moment in front of the tellers, she stared at the walls, the floor, and the ceiling, shifting from foot to foot. Perhaps she should get back to Mrs. Potts and the girls. Waiting to see the man she would see all evening seemed so silly, and yet she couldn't bring herself to leave.

It was a shameless infatuation she was laboring under, and she seemed to have less control over herself and her actions than she'd had in a long time. Nietzsche and Kierkegaard would both be disgusted with her, and yet she knew they wouldn't be surprised. After all, she was a woman in love and just knowing that in a few minutes she would hear Max's voice and he'd say her name made her heart flutter in her chest.

A little longer, and she was finally in front of him. Max looked up, recognized her, and his expression grew grave.

"Susan? Is everything all right?" he asked. "Has something happened to the girls?"

She shook her head, realizing this wasn't the magical, romantic meeting of lovers stealing a moment in the day she had imagined it would be. She had truly scared him by showing up unexpectedly. In her defense, she'd never read romantic novels. Perhaps she should. They might provide a road map for how this was supposed to play out.

"No, nothing like that," she said. "It's just..." She cast about for something to say and decided to go with recent events. "We, that is the girls and I, wanted to buy some seeds for the kitchen garden, and I forgot to ask if it was all right. I have the girls and Mrs. Potts in the store right now, choosing which seeds to buy, and I thought I should at least speak to you about it."

Max's frown faded, and he smiled. "It's fine. You can buy any you like. Only no Brussel sprouts. I think they're disgusting."

"Good, because I agree," Susan said with a smile. "I'll see you later?"

"You can count on it, my love," he said, taking her hand that she'd laid on the counter. "You can bet your life on it."

Susan sighed at his touch and, remembering herself, blinked and pulled herself together. Max seemed just as affected by her presence and seemed loath to let her hand go. He did, however, and she headed to the door. All eyes in the bank were on them, and Susan felt her cheeks redden.

"Newlyweds," one woman said with a smile. "It's so sweet."

Just then the door flew open. It hit Susan in the shoulder, pushing her off balance. She stumbled.

Suddenly, someone grabbed her and pushed her face-first into the wall.

"All right, you scum-suckers! No one make any sudden moves, and some of y'all will make it out of here alive!" a gruff voice said.

The rough hands holding Susan turned her around and threw her to the floor. Susan landed amid a tangle of other patrons who had simply come into the bank to conduct their business. Standing over them were men with bandanas tied over the bottom halves of their faces. What she found her eyes focusing on the most, however, were the pistols pointed at each and every one of them.

CHAPTER 13

Susan picked herself up to a sitting position and helped an old man, his hair gray and his face wrinkled, to find his spectacles that had skittered across the floor. Another man, also a customer, picked them up and handed them back. He received a blow to the head with the back of a pistol for his kindness.

"What is wrong with you?" Susan demanded, her temper flaring.

The man who had hit the customer in the head raised his pistol to bash it against her skull too. Susan glared at him, petrified beyond sense, and yet not wanting to give him the satisfaction of seeing her flinch.

"Enough! We don't need to hit everyone!" the gruff voice said. Its owner turned, and Susan recognized his white-blond hair. She'd seen the man outside a few minutes ago. "Now, everyone pipe down. Tellers, if you would come and join us here in the front, I think we can conduct our business and be gone shortly."

Susan watched, her heart pounding in her chest as Max left his counter and came into the throng of people. He moved to be near her, taking her hand in his as they crouched on the floor.

"All right, now that we're one big happy family, let's get to it," the man said. He scanned the group in front of him. "Where is the bank manager? I understand, from previous experience, that he is the only person here with the keys to the vault."

No one said a thing. No one moved. Max held Susan's hand tightly, never taking his eyes off the speaker.

The gruff-voiced man sighed. "No manager today? We choose the wrong day?" He leaned forward, waving his gun around. Susan noticed a rather large knife sheath on his belt and wondered what on earth he'd need that for.

"Tell me, Toady," he said, turning to one of his men who had bulging eyes. "How many banks you know of open up for business with no one on the premises who can open the vault? How many?"

Toady looked over at his boss and smiled, making him look very like his nickname. "None, boss," he said. "Not a one."

Gruff Man nodded and turned his attention to the group of huddled, frightened people in front of him. Susan gripped Max's hand tightly, hoping not to catch the man's eye. She knew what deer must feel like when a pack of wolves was surrounding them. Her heart thudded in her chest, and she couldn't seem to breathe properly.

"Toady here says not a one," Gruff Man said. His eyes roamed over the people again, and Max glared at him.

Susan wanted to grab Max, tell him to put his head down and not draw attention to himself. Surely, someone else at the bank would be able to help these ruffians and get them out of the bank.

"I'm gonna give you one chance to come forward, whichever of you has the keys, and there will be no repercussions," Gruff Man said.

He waited and Max shifted. "I have to go," he whispered to Susan.

"But," she began.

Max opened the hand not holding hers and showed her a group of three keys on a ring. She held his hand tight, stiffening as though she could turn to stone and protect him if she could just keep him with her.

Gruff Man sighed. "Truly, I was hoping not to have to do this. But I guess you want a scramble, you gotta break some eggs. So, whose egg will it be?" He nodded to one of his men, and a woman was hauled up by her hair with a piercing scream. "How about this egg?" the man asked. "She looks good for cracking."

Max sighed and, kissing Susan's cheek very briefly, raised his hand. Susan shook her head. She tried to grab him, but Max stood, leaving her on the floor as tears threatened to rise and overwhelm her. She was about to lose him; she could feel it.

"I can open the safe for you," Max said. "Just let Mrs. Turner go."

Just then a loud voice rent the air.

"All right! Listen up in there! We know you're robbing the bank. We take a dim view of this, so how about you fellas come on out and we talk this through? Huh?"

The man referred to as Toady grabbed Max and hauled him up. He held Max's one arm behind his back at a painful angle, and Max gasped.

"Who is that addressing us?" Gruff Man asked.

"It's Sheriff Dodge," Max said.

"How many men he got?" the other man asked.

Max shook his head. "Hard to say. He's got one deputy, but a lot of the store owners are volunteers."

"You tellin' me porky pies, boy?" Gruff Man asked.

"He's telling you the truth," the old man who still crouched next to Susan said. "We don't know how many men Dodge has right now. Why don't you ask him?"

With horrible violence, one of Gruff Man's minions hit the old man in the chest, and he fell back into Susan.

"Stop it!" she yelled. "Can't you just go and take your money and leave? None of these people deserve you hitting them!"

"Well, well, a good Samaritan," Gruff man said. "I'll deal with you later."

"No, you won't!" Max said. "I'll get you what you want. I can open the safe. But the deal's off if you hurt her. You got it? You leave my wife alone."

"Now that is a wonderful little nugget, ain't it? She's your wife," Gruff Man said. "I think this might be worth my attention."

"Hey! You in there!" came Sheriff Dodge's voice again. "Come out. We got this place surrounded. You ain't getting out alive unless you come now."

Gruff Man laughed. All his men joined in.

"Thinks this is our first rodeo," he said. "Ah, how I do love the law enforcement in these little towns." He shook his head theatrically.

"Funny," one of his men said.

"Okay, Georgie, we got us a player," Gruff Man said, turning to another of his men. "Take this one to the back to open the safe. Me and this woman, we gonna have ourselves a little fun in the manager's office."

"No!" Max cried, digging his heels in and not moving. "I won't do a thing for you if you touch so much as a hair on her head!"

"Tough guy!" Gruff Man said. "Listen to me nicely now; she's coming with me, and you're going with

Georgie, and should there be any funny business, she won't get back to you in anything but a nice pine box. So, off you go..." He waved his gun in the direction of the back of the bank. "Go on!"

Susan watched Max's expression and saw how angry he was as Gruff Man came to stand right in front of her. She didn't like the look in the man's eyes.

"I'll be fine," she said.

Gruff Man grabbed her arm painfully, making her cry out.

Max threw his head back and hit Georgie in the face. The man's nose erupted in blood. Free, he dashed at Gruff Man, meaning to hit him in the stomach with his shoulder. Toady stepped into Max's path at the last second and, taking the blow for his boss, made an "ooof" sound and crashed into the front window.

Susan hardly dared to breathe. Gruff Man wheeled her around so she could watch the action and held her close to him. There was no moving now. He had her firmly in his clutches. Panic threatened to engulf her. She was a rabbit cornered by a fox.

It all happened so quickly, so unexpectedly. She could only stare. She should help Max, somehow, but as she realized this, it was already too late. Gruff Man had her. He held something hard to her ribs. A gun.

"Hey!" he called. "You forgetting something? I got your woman. You want her to live, you better stop hitting Toady! I know he's a bit of a rough sort, but you look like a fine gentleman. So how about you start acting like one?"

Max froze in the act of punching Toady in the face. Toady threw him off and landed a few punches of his own on Max's face and his stomach.

"Got a lot of fizz for a banker," Gruff Man said to Susan. "No wonder you like him." Then, turning his attention to Max, who had his hands up in surrender, he said, "Come on, boy. Get me my money and you can go home and pretend this never happened." He regarded Max's rapidly bruising face and split lip, where a trickle of blood was oozing down his chin. "Well, in a couple of weeks, you can. Jefferson, take this man to the back, and let's get this done!"

Another man came forward and shoved the barrel of his shotgun in Max's back.

"How do I know you won't do anything to her?" Max asked.

"You don't," Gruff Man said, wrapping an arm around Susan and holding her back to him. His gun moved from her ribs to be held visibly against her temple. The cold of the barrel was a shock, and Susan sucked in an involuntary breath. "You just gotta trust me."

Susan didn't like the sound of this. She looked out over the sea of frightened faces of the bank customers and knew there would be no help there. It was up to her and Max to make sure that they made it back to their girls and Mrs. Potts. What must they be thinking? By now they must know something horrible was happening at the bank. Oh, poor Alyssa and Cassia. If anything happened, they would be all alone in the world. This was terrible.

That thought brought panic to Susan. She had to get free and get out of there. She was the closest thing to a mother these girls had. And their father was risking his life right now, trying to appease these people. And what if they decided this wasn't going to work out? That they couldn't leave all these witnesses? What then?

Dear God, please help us all get out of here safely!

Gruff Man seemed unsatisfied with waiting in the front of the bank, and with Susan walking backward, he dragged her around the counter and through a door to Mr. Morgan's office. It had a large glass window in one wall that let the banker take private meetings and keep an eye on the goings-on in the bank at the same time.

The robber shoved her into one of the visitor's chairs in front of the desk. "Don't move, okay? I'm not quite as quick a shot as Doc Halliday, but I'm right up there. You might make two steps before I blow your brains all over the wall. You got me?"

She nodded.

Gruff Man stuck his head out through the door and called, "Hey, Silvertongue, you go talk to the law through the door. Make them back off."

"You got it, boss," the man he'd called Silvertongue said before scampering to the door and opening it a crack. There were only two men watching the customers now, Georgie and Toady, but that didn't seem to make any difference. The rest of the customers were so petrified they were cowering, keeping their heads low and not looking at anyone. Mrs. Turner was whimpering, and the old man they'd hit was unconscious on the floor with no one looking after him.

Susan turned back to stare at the wall behind Mr. Morgan's desk as Gruff Man stuck his head back into the room.

Through the open doorway, she could hear the man called Silvertongue speaking, but what he was saying was a mystery. She couldn't make out the actual words.

How long would it take Max to get to the bank vault? She knew it was in the basement. He'd told her that much, but anything else was a mystery. And what would happen then? What would Jefferson do to him once the vault was open? To keep herself from going mad waiting, she decided to strike up a conversation.

Turning in her seat, she addressed Gruff Man. "I suppose you subscribe to a Machiavellian view of the world," she said.

Gruff Man shifted, pointing the gun at her from the doorway. "A what?"

"Niccolò Machiavelli," Susan said. "The sixteenth-century philosopher? He said, 'Is it better to be loved more than feared, or feared more than loved? The reply is that one ought to be both feared and loved, but as it is difficult for the two to go together, it is much safer to be feared than loved, if one of the two has to be wanting.' You clearly follow his way of thinking."

"You don't say?" Gruff Man said. "How do you know about this?"

"I study philosophy," Susan said. "It's very interesting. Perhaps if you spent a little more time with books instead of guns…"

Gruff Man laughed. "Perhaps if your parents taught you about silence, I wouldn't be fighting the urge to shoot you in the head."

"Or perhaps you'd like to tell me why you're so keen to rob this bank? It is a little bank in a tiny town. Surely you could have gone to Salem or one of the bigger towns?" Susan asked. "Wouldn't it be worth your while? I mean, how much can you possibly get out of this bank?"

"It ain't about that," Gruff Man said, moving into the room to stand right in front of her. "This money is rightly mine. Well, some of it anyway, but I figure they owe me grievance pay. So, now that I told you, can you shut your trap for a minute?"

Susan nodded, but the silence wasn't good for her. It rolled around in her head, and she began to panic.

What if she never saw Max in this life again? She'd just found love, just found happiness with a lovely family with two wonderful little girls. If all that was taken from her now? What then? How were they going to get out of this alive? She couldn't see a way, and it turned her blood cold.

In this state of abject fear, she found her thoughts turning to God. With her heart in her throat and acid bile rising, she prayed. Susan prayed for Max and for Alyssa and Cassia. She prayed for everyone stuck in this nightmare with her. She could only hope God would hear her.

Just then there was a crash, and the front window burst into shards that flew through the air. Gruff Man moved like a cobra, striking so fast Susan didn't have time to react at all. He hauled her to her feet and dragged her in front of him, using her as a shield. A man came through the window and was shot in the side. He went down. Another came through and another.

Gruff Man's men were shooting, and others outside were returning fire. A stray bullet shattered the glass window in front of her, and Susan felt several bits slice into her flesh. Gruff Man grunted. He must have felt one or two as well.

He held the gun to her head.

Suddenly, a man was in the doorway. Gruff Man shot at him. Bam! Bam! Bam! Three bullets fired, and three bullets missed. The man ducked down behind the wall.

"Come on now! We got your men down. It's just you left, Gorman," the man called. "Come on out."

The man Susan had called Gruff Man and who was really called Gorman shook his head. "Nah! I think I'll stay here until you agree that me and this little filly get safe conduct out of here."

"Ain't happening," the man said.

A slice of the man's hat appeared through the now-shattered window, and Gorman took a shot at it. Bam! Click! Click! He was out of bullets.

Gorman swore and dropped the gun.

This was her moment. Susan shifted in his grip but found he had something cold, hard, and sharp at her throat in seconds. The knife she'd seen in that huge sheath. She stopped moving.

"I don't want to shoot you, Gorman!" the man called. "But I will."

Gorman yelled something obscene, and then the man rolled out from behind the wall and took a shot. It was over in seconds. Susan felt a sharp pain in her left shin as though someone had hit her with a lead pipe. She went down and clocked her head on something, filling it with pain.

For a moment, stars appeared and burst before her eyes as the world erupted around her. Someone was screaming in pain, and it wasn't Susan. She knew that because darkness was growing in the corners of her vision, and soon it enveloped her.

When her head cleared, someone was holding her. Susan blinked. It was Mrs. Turner.

"What happened?" she asked.

"Deputy Baxter," Mrs. Turner said. She was a mousy woman with prominent front teeth when she smiled. "He shot that horrible robber in the leg, and it seems his bullet nicked you. Dr. Jackson says you'll be fine though. See, all bandaged up."

Susan sat up, her head aching. She saw that her left calf had a bandage wrapped around it. "And my head?"

"Seems you hit it on the edge of the desk as you fell," Mrs. Turner said.

Things were coming back to Susan, and she started in alarm. "Max! Where is Max?"

He had to have made it. He had to be okay. She couldn't breathe! Where was he?

"It's okay, calm down!" Mrs. Turner said. "He's just over there talking to the deputy."

Susan looked past her, and at first, she couldn't find him. But then someone moved, and she saw him. It was Max. His right hand was bandaged, but he looked whole. He turned at that moment and smiled at her. In a flash he came over and wrapped his arms around her.

"Oh! You're all right!" she cried, tears of relief flooding down her cheeks. "Thank you, Lord!"

He smiled. "Yes, I'm fine. And you?"

"I'm fine," Susan said, trying to wipe her face ineffectually.

After a couple of minutes, Max helped Susan up, and she found the world was a very different place. Gorman and his men were gone, and a man with a black doctor's bag was bent over an older man lying on the floor in a pool of blood.

"Sheriff Dodge," Max said. "He came in through the window, and his deputy came through the back. I let him in when I got that ruffian off me. Everything is going to be fine."

"But he's shot," Susan said.

"Only in the hip," the doctor said over his shoulder. "He should be all right. I think we can move him now. Someone help me get him to my surgery."

And that was it.

A little later, Susan and Max made their way out of the bank. She was still a little shaky, and her leg throbbed. Her head was of larger concern, and Dr. Jackson said she should come by his surgery the next day, and he'd make sure she was fine. For now, she needed some rest. Best news of all, she and Max could go home.

Mrs. Potts and the girls were beside themselves with worry. When they saw Max and Susan appear out of the bank, the girls rushed them, crying. Susan and Max enveloped them in hugs, and even Mrs. Potts was dragged in. Then the happy troupe made their slow way home, thankful to have each other in one piece.

EPILOGUE

March 1871

Sheriff Dodge spent two weeks in bed, and during that time, his young deputy, Adam Baxter, spent his time solving the case of the bank robbery. It turned out that the Gruff Man's name was Hank Adamson, and he'd been an employee at the local mine for the last five years. However, after being sacked for beating a fellow miner into a coma, he was bitter. He hatched a plan to steal the wages and make off with them.

Having managed to steal them from the Crystal Lake bank, he decided he'd do it again when the mine moved to Bear Creek's bank.

Susan was just thankful she and Max had gotten out safely, especially when he told her how he'd overpowered the ruffian and opened the back door for the deputy. It was such a brave, crazy thing to do, she didn't know whether to kiss him or yell at him. Of course, he'd gone for the kiss.

All this was weeks ago, and yet it still seemed fresh in her mind. Just looking at her little family made Susan relive it often, and often she had to ask God for help. It seemed her relationship with the big man upstairs was somewhat repaired. She would never give up her philosophy, but she figured if Kierkegaard could have both, then so could she.

It was Sunday, and they were at the farm. The lambs were growing like little weeds, and the girls were overcome with delight when they were allowed to stroke them. The fwhole family was sitting on blankets under some trees, having a picnic, and it was a lovely way to spend an afternoon with dappled sunshine warming them.

"I'm so glad you're all here," Emily said. She was beaming. "Apart from the news that Kyle and Sadie's house is almost finished and they will be moving out from under my feet in the next couple of weeks, we have something else we want to tell you all."

"Well?" Sadie asked. "What is it?"

She was lying with her head on Kyle's arm as he played with her hair.

Susan lay on her stomach with Max next to her, both with a glass of small cider before them.

Emily looked at Tony and took his hand. He smiled at her and kissed her hand.

"No way?" Susan said as she guessed what Emily's news was.

Emily frowned at her. "How did you guess?"

Susan shrugged. "It's obvious."

"What is?" Sadie asked. "Susan! I demand one of you tell me what's going on."

"Well, Em, it's your circus," Susan said with a naughty grin.

Emily's smile was huge. "I'm pregnant," she said.

"No!" Sadie exclaimed. "Really?"

Emily nodded.

"Congratulations," Max said, shaking Tony's hand. "Your life will never be the same."

Tony laughed and shrugged. "To be honest, I didn't think it would happen this soon."

Susan hugged her sister. "Congratulations. You'll make a wonderful mother."

Emily beamed. "I hope so."

As the joy wound around her, Susan knew she'd found her place in the world. She was a mother, a wife, and a teacher, and she could be all those things and more. She had a wonderful man by her side, who loved her for who she was, without wanting her to change. All in all, life was truly blessed, and she knew the reason why.

Thank you, Lord.

To continue enjoying Six Sisters For Bear Creek Complete Series. (6 Book Series)

KATIE WYATT & ADA OAKLEY

HISTORICAL MAIL ORDER BRIDE WESTERN ROMANCE

SIX SISTERS FOR BEAR CREEK

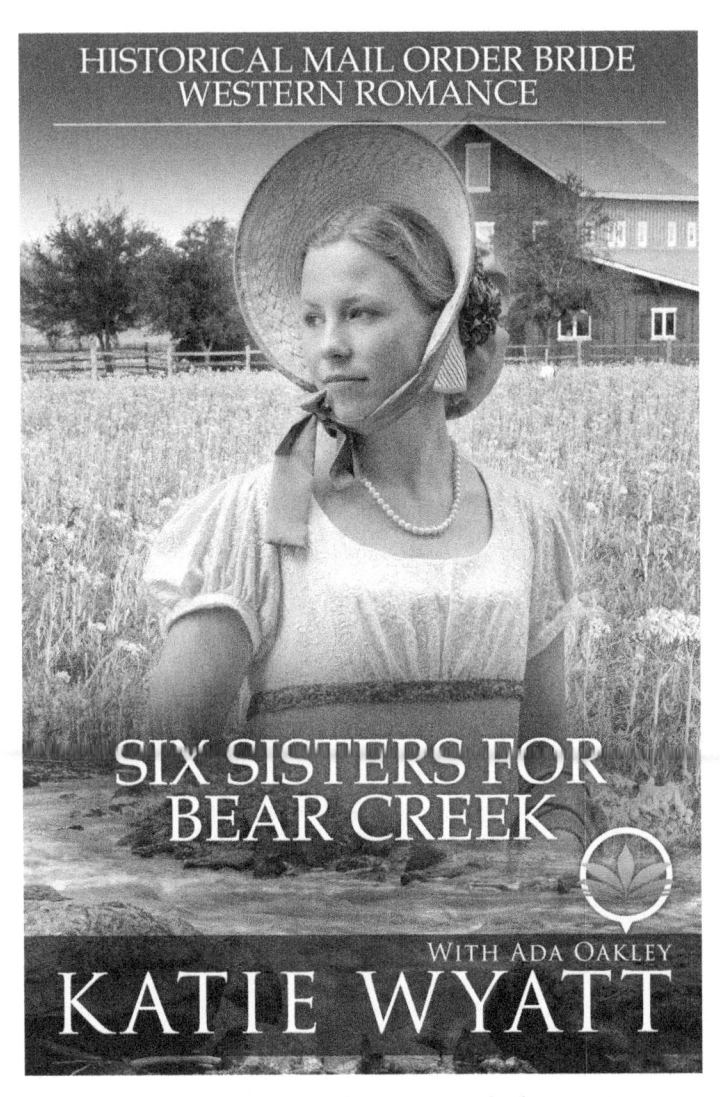

With Ada Oakley

KATIE WYATT

Katie Wyatt Six Sisters For Bear Creek

SUSAN'S TRUTH

Royce Cardiff Publishing House presents other wonderful clean, wholesome and inspiring romance short stories titles for your entertainment. Many are value boxset and as always FREE to Kindle Unlimited readers.

COMPLETE SERIES
Sweet Western Romance

KATIE WYATT, BRENDA CLEMMONS AND ELLEN ANDERSON

katie wyatt box set complete series

Sweet Frontier Cowboys Complete Series Collection (A Novel Christian Romance Series)

Mega Box Set Complete Series By Katie Wyatt

Katie Wyatt Mega Box Set Series (12 Mega Box Set Series)

THANK YOU SO MUCH FOR READING MY BOOK. I sincerely hope you enjoyed every bit reading it. I had fun creating it and will surely create more.

Your positive reviews are very helpful to other reader, it only takes a few moments. They can be left at Amazon.

www.amazon.com/Katie-Wyatt/e/B011IN7AF0

WANT FREE BOOKS EVERY WEEK? WHO DOESN'T!

. . .

Become a preferred reader and we'll not only send you free reads, but you'll also receive updates about new releases.

So you'll be among the first to dive into our latest new books, full of adventure, heartwarming romances, and characters so real they jump off the page.

It's absolutely free and you don't need to do anything at all to qualify except go to.

PREFERRED READ FREE READS

http:/katieWyattBooks.com/readersgroup

ABOUT THE AUTHORS

KATIE WYATT IS 25% AMERICAN SIOUX INDIAN. Born and raised in Arizona, she has traveled and camped extensively through California, Arizona, Nevada, Mexico, and New Mexico. Looking at the incredible night sky and the giant Saguaro cacti, she has dreamed of what it would be like to live in the early pioneer times.

Spending time with a relative of the great Wyatt Earp, also named Wyatt Earp, Katie was mesmerized and inspired by the stories he told of bygone times. This historical interest in the old West became the inspiration for her Western romance novels.

Her books are a mixture of actual historical facts and events mixed with action and humor, challenges and adventures. The characters in Katie's clean romance novels draw from her own experiences and are so real that they almost jump off the pages. You feel like you're walking beside them through all the ups and downs of their lives. As the stories unfold, you'll find yourself both laughing and crying. The endings will never fail to leave you feeling warm inside.

ADA OAKLEY IS AN AMERICAN-BORN ITALIAN, who has lived most of her life in Dallas Texas and has traveled to many countries. She has been an avid reader and a lover of western movies since her teenage years, so she decided to pursue a writing career.

Ada loves writing Western Romance and Mail Order Bride stories about the courageous women who traveled alone to the Wild West with nothing but hope and strong faith in God.

Her inspirations are her dogs and three lovely cats! So if you're up to reading an excellent feel good clean romance story, her stories are highly recommended.

Made in the USA
Coppell, TX
23 May 2021

56163918R00090